"Lacy, I told you to get out of this heat." Clint's spurs clinked ominously as he stepped toward her.

She plunked a hand on her hip and met his deadly glare. "And I told you I had to finish painting today, Clint." *Goodness, but the man was gorgeous.*

"Either you come down off that roof, or I'm coming up and hauling you down."

The men grouped at the foot of the ladder looked from Clint to Lacy.

"Two things. One—I'd like to see you try hauling me down from here. And two—what are *they* doing here?"

"*My men* are going to finish the job for you. Now come on down. Or I'm warning you, I'm coming up."

That man had to be the orneriest one she'd ever met in her life. Not many men stood up to her for long. There was no sense in letting him know how much she appreciated his coming to her rescue. Or how much she needed rescuing.

DEBRA CLOPTON

was a 2004 Golden Heart finalist in the inspirational category. *The Trouble with Lacy Brown* is her debut novel. She and her two wonderful sons make their home in a small town in Texas surrounded by a loving family and a host of fantastic friends.

DEBRA CLOPTON

The Trouble With Lacy Brown

Steeple Hill®

Published by Steeple Hill Books™

STEEPLE HILL BOOKS

Steeple
Hill®

ISBN 0-373-87328-X

THE TROUBLE WITH LACY BROWN

Copyright © 2005 by Debra Clopton

All rights reserved. Except for use in any review, the reproduction
or utilization of this work in whole or in part in any form by any
electronic, mechanical or other means, now known or hereafter
invented, including xerography, photocopying and recording, or in
any information storage or retrieval system, is forbidden without
the written permission of the editorial office, Steeple Hill Books,
233 Broadway, New York, NY 10279 U.S.A.

All characters in this book have no existence outside the imagination of
the author and have no relation whatsoever to anyone bearing the same
name or names. They are not even distantly inspired by any individual
known or unknown to the author, and all incidents are pure invention.

This edition published by arrangement with Steeple Hill Books.

® and TM are trademarks of Steeple Hill Books, used under license.
Trademarks indicated with ® are registered in the United States Patent
and Trademark Office, the Canadian Trade Marks Office and in other
countries.

www.SteepleHill.com

Printed in U.S.A.

Now the end of the commandment is charity
out of a pure heart, and of a good conscience,
and of faith unfeigned.

—*1 Timothy* 1:5

This book is dedicated with all my love to my husband, Wayne, my hero, my best friend, the love of my life, the father of our sons, Chase and Kris. Until I see you again...I'll be missing you.

1955–2003

You are always and forever in my heart and on my mind.

Prologue

Perched on the door of her topless pink Caddy, Lacy Brown surveyed the sleepy town she'd driven all night and five hundred miles to wake up.

At six in the morning the town looked comatose. It was a pitiful sight, an odd assortment of brick and clapboard buildings staggered down both sides of the deserted street. The place had seen better days. At least Lacy hoped it had; it didn't look as though things could get much worse.

All the buildings were in desperate need of paint. The sidewalks were made from planks, *real planks,* half of which were curled up on the edges or missing. Every aspect of the town screamed for help, but the vacant windows said the most. Smeared with years of grime, they greeted Lacy like eyes lost in absolute despair.

From the pocket of her worn jeans she dug the crumpled newspaper clipping that had changed her life.

"Small Texas town of Mule Hollow—where the cowboys grow tall but the women aren't at all; WIVES NEEDED…."

Lacy had always been drawn to anyone in distress. And goodness, this was an entire town sending out an S.O.S.

So here she was at the break of dawn staring down Mule Hollow's Main Street.

Its appearance tugged at her heart. It was as if the town had seen one too many people drive down this road and keep right on going.

She understood that feeling all too well, but pushing the thought away, she concentrated on her mission. She closed her eyes as the soft whisper of a morning breeze touched her skin and she felt…a heartbeat?

A spark.

That was it! Her eyelids lifted to the warm touch of dawn peeking over the rooftops.

She understood.

Mule Hollow was holding its breath.

Wishing.

Waiting for someone to come along and pump life back into its tired old buildings.

Peace flowed over her.

She'd been right in coming, right in listening to the Lord's call.

Oh, Father, thank You for leading me here. Thank You, thank You, thank You.

Chapter One

"Rise and shine, Sheri, we made it to Mule Hollow." Lacy Brown leaned over and slapped the pair of pointed, high-heeled boots propped on the dusty dashboard of her classic pink Caddy.

The rumpled heap that was her friend and partner opened one eye. "No, not now," she grumbled. "I just started dreaming about handsome cowboys fighting over me."

"Why dream?" Lacy practically sang with enthusiasm. "Open your eyes and look around."

With her hair resembling Rod Stewart's on a bad hair day, Sheri plopped her feet to the floorboard one at a time, pushed up to a sitting position and gaped at Mule Hollow. "You're joking. *Right?*"

"Isn't it wonderful?" Lacy said, flinging her arms

open wide. From her perch on the car's door she felt on top of the world.

"Wonderful. Lace, are we looking at the same view? *Look at this place.*"

"No, no, no, don't go all negative on me, Sheri. Look again. Really look." Overflowing with excitement, Lacy jumped to her feet on the Caddy's seat. "Picture all these sad, colorless buildings painted a different shade of the rainbow. Like…like one of those weird ski villages in Colorado—only brighter." She grasped Sheri by the shoulders and met her eye-to-eye. "We prayed about opening our own business. And you know when I read that classified ad, God gave me a vision. I'm telling you, girlfriend, whoever placed that ad is watching the same movie I'm watching. If we open it, they'll come. I know it. I feel it in my heart."

"Girlfriend—" Sheri took a deep breath "—this is no cornfield and you are *not* Kevin Costner."

Lacy dropped back onto the edge of the door. "Nope, I'm not Kevie-baby, but when single women read about all these lonesome, long-legged cowboys pinning away for true love—they're coming. All kinds of man-hunters from all walks of life. Who knows, there may be hundreds."

Sheri rolled her eyes, but grinned.

That's all the encouragement Lacy needed to rattle on. "No joke. Some gals will come to marry, some to play. Either way, when the courtin' starts, where is the first place those gals are gonna head?"

Sheri bit her lip to hide her smile, and then gave in. "Straight to *Heavenly Inspirations,*" she drawled, "Where love is in the air *and* the hair!"

"Yup, yup, yup, that's what I'm saying," Lacy chirped. "With me styling their hair and you sculpting their nails, not only are we going to be independent, self-supporting businesswomen, we are going to get the opportunity to tell each and every one of those ladies what the Lord has done for us." Lacy's eyes twinkled. "There absolutely couldn't be anything better than that!"

Sheri started chuckling and dramatically slapped a hand to her chest. "Okay, Moses, I give up. God told you to come here and far be it for me to get in *His* way. We both know you're the one with the direct line to His office, I'm just along for the ride." She paused rubbed her eyes and stretched her arms heavenward. "But, friend of mine—" she yawned "—we have to take a time-out now and find coffee, I'm dying here."

Sheri was right, it had been a long five-hundred-mile drive through the night. Lacy slid behind the steering wheel, then rammed the gearshift into drive, all in one swift motion. "Coffee it is. I have to say, you do look as though you could use a few cups." She had to dodge a pillow as it was slammed into her shoulder.

Swinging the pink Caddy to the right she aimed it

toward a building she'd spied at the end of the street, where a couple of beat-up pickup trucks were parked in front. "The real estate agent said there was a diner of sorts on Main Street. Mmm-hmm, this is it," she mused, swerving into an angled parking space in front of the building. A worn sign proclaimed Sam's Pharmaceuticals And Diner. To the side some small print had been added. Eat At Your Own Peril 6 a.m.-8 p.m.

Lacy stomped hard on the brakes. While her buddy peeled herself off the dashboard, Lacy scrambled over the closed door Dukes of Hazzard-style to survey the dilapidated building up close. She paused when a striped cat hissed at her from its hiding place beneath the plank sidewalk. "What's up, little friend?" Lacy asked, bending down to get a better look at the frightened creature. Obviously not tamed, it backed farther away into the shadows as it continued to emit unearthly noises. "I hope you're not the welcoming committee," she chuckled softly.

From the car, Sheri moaned, "It should be a sin to be so perky. Watching you, no one would believe we drove all night to get here."

Lacy stood and turned toward her friend. "I'm too excited to be tired. Don't you feel it?" She closed her eyes again. The tugging at her heart was stronger now. She felt a whisper of hope. Opening her eyes, she looked straight at Sheri. "This is our future. Our destiny."

Sheri pulled on the door latch. "Only you could read a little ad about a podunk town needing would-be-wives and see your future. *And* hear God's call at the same time."

"*Our* future." Lacy stuck her hand on her hip. "You have a stake in this enterprise also."

"Oh, yeah, my life savings," Sheri retorted. "All three hundred and thirty-four cents' worth."

Ignoring Sheri's teasing, Lacy turned, stepped up on the plank sidewalk and swished across to the weathered building. Lovingly she ran a hand over the rough wood. "You know you're just as excited about bringing this town to life as I am." Ignoring Sheri's complaints was habit. Early on in their lives, Sheri had been the straggler, so shy she could hardly look a person in the eyes. That fact had compelled them into friendship as elementary school kids. Lacy had taken it upon herself to pull Sheri off the sidelines, straight into the action. Because of that, Sheri's confidence had grown over the years and with it her ability to banter.

Tracing a finger along the wood Lacy lifted an eyebrow at her friend, "You know you can't wait to paint this dull, dry heap of wood."

"If this place only knew what you have in store for it, they'd roll up the sidewalks and lock the doors." Shaking her head Sheri strode to the door of Sam's. "I'm getting coffee. *Now.* Before you get us thrown out of town and I have to wait another couple of hours for the next chance."

Lacy watched her not-so-shy-anymore friend stride through the diner's heavy swinging door. Where had that timid little girl gone? Lacy took all the blame for having rubbed off on Sheri, but at least her friend had no fear of new places or new faces. And that was a good thing. With one last glance about, Lacy followed Sheri into the diner. It was definitely coffee time.

Inside the diner, the musty scent of age mingled with smells of pine floors, gumballs from children long grown and strong, fragrant coffee.

"Coffee," Sheri groaned to the older man behind the carved, wooden counter.

He reminded Lacy of a raisin. Small, slightly plump and wrinkled all over, he was so cute she had to fight the impulse to pinch him. Clearly that wouldn't be the right way to start a new relationship. She slid into the booth instead and held up two fingers. "Make that two, please."

She tugged her orange T-shirt from her skin and fanned herself. Riding five hundred miles with the top down made a body slightly sticky and smelly, too. But she loved her convertible and wouldn't take a new car for anything. Clean air blowing through her hair. That was the good life. Who cared about a few bugs here and there, in her teeth, in the eye…?

Tapping her fingers on the table she nodded at the

two ancient men hunched over a checkerboard in the corner by the window. So *they* were what early birds looked like.

"Hi," she called.

They nodded in acknowledgment and continued their game of checkers unmoved as Lacy surveyed the room. A jukebox in the corner snagged her attention, drawing her to investigate. Like everything else in the café, it was straight out of a decade before any she'd lived in. The box was covered with bright lights and filled with little records. It was irresistible.

Digging a nickel from her pocket she plopped it into the slot, selected her favorite, "Blue Suede Shoes," then strolled back to her table.

Thank You, Lord. Everything is perfect.

The explosive strains of Jerry Lee Lewis singing "Great Balls of Fire" blasted from the jukebox.

"Rattle my brain—Baabaaabie!" Sheri squealed along with the song. "Where's Elvis?"

Lacy shrugged, amazed at how well her friend knew her, even more amazed at how far Sheri's shyness had come since they were kids. "Beats me, that box must have a mind of its own."

"Ain't that the truth," Little Raisin Man said, coming around the counter to set two mugs of steaming coffee on their table. "That there's the only song that thang'll play." He shook his balding head, "I liked the song once, a long, *long* time ago. What can I get you gals to eat?"

Lacy stilled the rat-a-tat-tat of her hot pink finger-nails on the scarred pine tabletop. "Nothing for me, but thank you." Offering her hand in greeting, she smiled up at the darling man. "I'm Lacy Brown, and this is Sheri Marsh."

He wiped his hands on his white apron and shook Lacy's hand violently. "Sam's the name. What brings you gals to Mule Hollow?"

"Business. I'm opening the new hair salon."

Sam's expression didn't waver a smidge as his gaze slid to Sheri, and her brunette bird's nest, then volleyed back to rest once more on Lacy.

Glancing at her reflection in the mirror behind the counter, Lacy nearly fell off her chair. Her whipped cream-colored curls licked from beneath her ball cap like curdled milk on a hot day.

Sam, a real trooper, never blinked. "Figures," he said dryly, as if hair like theirs were a common occurrence. "The real estate agent told Adela you'd be here next week."

"I couldn't wait," Lacy explained, tapping her nails again. "Patience is not one of my strong points."

"Craziest thing I ever heard, this plan of the gals. You're the first, you know."

"We figured it," Sheri and Lacy said in unison.

"At least we hoped we were the first," added Lacy.

"By my calculations you might be the only. The women folk put out the ad-verd-is-ment. Not us." He sighed and shook his head as if that told the story in a nutshell.

It was obvious the only one in on this plan other than them was God. Lacy glanced at the checker players, who had abandoned their game to listen intently to their conversation. "By chance, would any of you nice gentlemen know which building out there is mine?"

Sam harrumphed. "Ain't been a building rented out in this town for pert near ten years. Everybody knows your building. It's here on Main Street down across from Pete's Feed-and-Seed. He'd be opening 'bout now. Can't miss it. Only other buildin' with cars out front."

Lacy stood. "Can you catch me later, Sheri? I have to see it."

"Sure, go ahead, check out your destiny. I'm going to sit right here, have another coffee and eat this fine man out of business." Sheri stretched and patted her stomach while grinning at Sam.

"Get ready, Sam, she's not kidding." Already Lacy was pushing through the swinging door, waving goodbye over her shoulder.

Standing on the sidewalk, she tugged the brim of her ball cap lower to shield her eyes against the rising sun's glare. It sat higher in the sky now, and with it a few more cars moved about. Down the street, she spotted a gas station that still boasted a red flying horse sign, clearly ancient. That sign was probably worth a pretty penny at a flea market or auction. But the real jewel of the town could be seen a bit farther down at the end of Main Street—a majestically rambling old house replete with towers, lightning rods and loads of promise. Now that would be worth some exploration, she thought. Then, tugging once more at the bib of her cap, she strode to her Caddy and vaulted over the convertible's door.

The familiar exhilaration filled her when she turned the key and the powerful old engine roared to life. That sound never ceased to thrill her with joy. This morning she was high on life and feeling great. She was pressing the gas pedal when the hissing started—right there between her feet! One minute she had everything under control and then *whamo,* she had a frantic cat clinging to her leg, claws buried in her flesh. Lacy screamed in pain, but managed to stomp the brake, jerking the car to a halt just as the crazy cat sprang at her with teeth bared and claws out!

Clint Matlock needed a shower, a couple of cups of Sam's thick coffee and a noose. It had been another sleepless night, trying to catch a bunch of thieving rustlers. He was mad enough to follow in his great-great-granddaddy's footsteps—hangin' 'em first and asking questions later.

Heading toward Sam's Diner he turned his Jeep onto Main Street and was surprised to see a strange car parked out front.

"Would ya look at that," he whistled, eyeing the ugliest pink convertible he'd ever seen. The ancient sedan was so big it dwarfed the slim woman standing beside it. A tiny, little thing, she had cotton-white hair that shot out from under a red ball cap in wild curls. Her back was to him as she looked down toward the old Howard estate, but there was no mistaking she was a woman. As he approached, she surprised him when she sprang over the closed door of the car and landed easily in the driver's seat.

Slowing his Jeep behind the vehicular monstrosity, he was swinging into the space beside the piece of junk when its engine roared to life. The next few moments went in slow motion as the pink bombshell blasted toward him, then halted abruptly. Clint reacted by slamming on his brakes, but his empty thermos rocketed into the floorboard, lodged between his boots, the brake and the gas pedal. He was wrestling to get it out of his way when he accidentally hit the gas. Like a torpedo being shot out of a nuclear submarine Clint's Jeep raced toward the other car.

The impact took Lacy by surprise. She had been in midscream, watching the terrified cat fly past her face and out of the Caddy when it happened. The metal-on-metal impact threw her into the steering wheel and she ricocheted back against the seat.

Startled, to say the least, she'd managed to get a glance over her shoulder while being thrashed about and nearly croaked at the sight of the Jeep now connected to her back bumper.

One minute it was a beautiful glorious morning, a morning of bright new beginnings, of wondrous dreams come true. Then her beloved baby's rear end was flattened on the grill of a dusty black Jeep, and her dreams crashed and burned in a flash.

She didn't have the funds for a mess up like this!

When the Caddy at last came to a shuddering halt, Lacy had her eyes squeezed tightly shut.

The air was filled with a popping, bubbling sound followed by an ominous hissing and the noxious scent of something burning. *Dear Lord, please don't let anyone be harmed.*

Carefully prying her eyes open, she peeked into the rearview to see who had rammed her. Stormy, dark eyes framed by black smoke filled the mirror. She stared, transfixed by the reflection. The cowboy owning the angry eyes lifted one hand and with his thumb, pushed his beat-up straw Stetson off his forehead. His gaze never wavered from where it held hers in the mirror.

Lacy knew she better start thinking, but she couldn't; that gaze had taken root in her brain.

Rooted to the seat of her Caddy she watched the man in her mirror unfold his long, long legs from the accordion-pleated Jeep. Oh, dear, she forgot everything. Even the cat and the need to figure out the mess she found herself in. The guy was good-looking, the manly take-your-breath-away kind of good-looking. "My, my—oh my..." she gasped. In the mirror she could tell that if he were a specimen of the cowboys this town had to offer, then her vision of success for Mule Hollow was way off base. Woo-hoo! The women of the world were in for such a treat.

He *was* something, all lanky and lean, chiseled in all the right spots, and those eyes...flashing anger, clouded in turmoil— She lost him in the rearview as he made his way toward her.

"Are you all right?" he asked from just over her left shoulder.

His low Texas drawl was slow and gravelly and sent her pulse skittering as she twisted in her seat to face him. Oh, myyy... Swallowing hard, she looked up and up.

"What were you thinking?" he continued, rubbing the bridge of his nose.

And what a fine nose it was—

"What were you thinking?" he repeated, holding his voice tightly in control.

Lacy knew that voice. It happened a lot when she was around. "Nothing," she squeaked. She hated squeaking.

"Lady, if you don't know how to drive this piece of junk, then you should keep it off the street."

"Now, wait just a minute," she huffed, forgetting the cat for a moment to take up for her car. "You hit *me*. And watch what you call my Caddy!" Nobody picked on her prized possession. Scooting up, she perched on the top of her seat and glared at the rude cowboy. *That a girl, Lace.* Ohhh…up close, he was better than ever, kind of reminded her of a thirty-something Tom Selleck, minus the mustache. His sandy, brown hair ruffled around the edges of his Stetson. His eyes were deep amber-brown, spiked with charcoal and gold, probably why they were so vivid with anger.

"This happens to be a classic. Why, Elvis drove a car identical to this one," she deadpanned, finding it hard to stay mad at a guy who was going to help her business flourish.

Why, if they'd use him as a poster child for the town, there would be a stampede of women rushing to settle in for the long haul.

Cowboy's scowl deepened. He placed his hands on his hips, squared his shoulders and let out a long, slow breath. With effort, she tore her gaze away to focus on her car and the damage to the rear bumper.

"It…it's true. This is a '58 Caddy," she stammered, vaulting from the car and landing lightly before Handsome Cowboy. Unsettled and nervous, she walked to the rear of her poor car for a better look and a distraction from *him*. The fender was crinkled and the bumper was smushed into a crooked smile. It would have to be fixed at some point, but thankfully her baby was still drivable. Thank goodness for the heavy metal of a '58.

Unfortunately, the same couldn't be said of the Jeep. It had a caved-in front grill, a crumpled fender and more smoke than she liked still hissing from beneath the crinkled hood. It sounded like that horrible cat. "I am so sorry," she sighed.

"Not as sorry as I am. I hope you have insurance," he said dryly.

Lacy swallowed hard. It was the dreaded *I* word. She loved to drive, she spent hours in her car and she'd had only two other accidents *that weren't her fault, either.* But her insurance company didn't care at this point whose fault the accidents were, because of all the people out there to have run into she'd been hit by drivers driving illegally without insurance! "Well, actually—"

"Wonderful."

Lacy's stomach started to churn. She forced her flustered mind to think fast. One more claim against her insurance and she was in a crack without a shovel. Canceled! Hasta la vista, baby. No questions asked.

"Got a problem here, Clint?"

Lacy pivoted around and found she was staring at another very broad chest. This one belonged to an impossibly taller man in uniform. She had to tilt her head back in order to see all of him. Guess that ad wasn't lying about those guys being tall.

"Ma'am," the giant said, tipping his gray Stetson at her. "Seems you've had a little mishap."

"Brady. Irresponsible woman blared out of the parking space and rammed me—"

"I did not," Lacy objected. "Sheriff, it's true I pressed the accelerator because this cat attacked me, but I slammed on the brakes. I was already stopped when he snuck up on me. One minute he wasn't there. The next, wham! Right behind me. I'm sure it has happened to you before—well, maybe not. But anyway, a horn would have been nice!"

"What? Lady, you all but ran me down. Who had time to honk? One minute you were blasting out at me, the next you were stopped. All that starting and stopping caused my thermos to get tangled in the pedals."

"Aha! You *did* run into me."

Handsome Hunk took a step toward her, Lacy puffed her chest out and took a step forward. So there they stood, as eye-to-eye as her height could make it—but she was hanging in there for the count. She even thought her bravado was intimidating him a bit until he looked down his nicely tapered nose with his molten brown eyes, and chuckled.

Chuckled! "Why are you laughing?"

"Because this is absurd. Who are you anyway?"

"Lacy Brown," she enunciated very slowly.

"The trouble with you, Lacy Brown, is you don't know when you're whupped."

Lacy bristled. "Cowboy, I've never been whupped in my life. And I certainly don't intend to start now. You don't have a case."

A spattering of laughter broke out from the small crowd that had gathered. Lacy turned her attention to the nice giant standing quietly to the side. "Now, Sheriff—"

"Brady," he drawled.

Lacy smiled and shook his offered hand. "Brady, I'm new in town and don't mean to cause trouble. There must be some settlement we can agree on."

"Lacy," Sheri gasped, walking out of the café. "What's going on?"

"N-nothing. Just meeting the locals." She was squeaking again.

Sheri eyed the damage to both automobiles. "So, I see the ding machine is at it again."

"Ding machine!" echoed Clint the Cowboy.

Lacy glared at Sheri.

"What about a ding machine?" Sheriff Brady asked, crossing his arms over his wide chest.

"What about insurance?" Cowboy Clint asked, cocking his head to one side.

His smoking gaze roamed slowly over her and suddenly her heart started banging against her ribs.

"Well, I don't—"

"Figures," he drawled.

"What's that supposed to mean?" She felt very unsettled by the way he was looking at her. But even more so by the way it was affecting her, even as her heart sank at the thought of how much her insurance company disliked her.

"It means that anyone who would drive a car like that wouldn't have insurance."

"Why, cowboy, you're a snob." He was just assuming that her insurance problems were her fault.

"I certainly am not."

"Yes, you are. You decided that because I drive a car you don't like, that I wouldn't have insurance."

He raised an eyebrow. "You *don't* have insurance."

Lacy tapped her fingers on her thigh and glanced around at the expectant, slightly intrigued expressions watching her. Even Sheriff Brady was scratching his chin and taking in the spectacle she and Cowboy Clint were making. "I never said I didn't have insurance." You as good as don't have any. You can't use it, she thought miserably. "You see, the point is—"

"That you caved in the front of my Jeep and you don't have insurance. Therefore you're going to have to pay up. Out of your pocket."

Out of her pocket. Things were not going well for Lacy. True, he had hit her, but the cat was the real culprit here and it was nowhere to be seen. She glanced from Clint to Sheriff Brady, who seemed completely oblivious to his duties, instead, content to enjoy the show. She had a couple of problems. What little money she had was earmarked for the opening of her salon. Without it, all her dreams would go down the tubes. But without her insurance, she couldn't drive. She had to drive. Could her insurance company cancel her policy even if it wasn't her fault?

Licking her lips, she did some fast thinking. After she opened her salon she could fit the repairs into her budget if she had to, and maybe they wouldn't have to make a claim on her Caddy, just the Jeep. If only Clint the Cowboy would have patience and give her the time, which he should since *he* had run into *her.* She didn't mind paying for the damages to her car, because of the cat, but who did this guy think he was trying to railroad her into taking all the blame? This would not do at all. If there was one thing Lacy Brown didn't like, it was a bully.

"Where are my manners?" she asked, thinking it was time to turn the tables. "You know my complete name while I haven't had the honor. It's Clint—?"

Her gram, rest her soul, had always said her smile could melt bricks and buy gold. Holding out her hand, she smiled sweetly and waited for what seemed like forever. *I'm not trying to be deceptive, Lord. Really.*

Finally, after eyeing her hand like it was a rattler, Clint reached out and grasped it in a very firm handshake.

Lacy forgot everything.

"Matlock."

Busy assimilating the reaction to his touch, Lacy didn't understand the question. "W-what?" Her gaze dropped to their clasped hands, then back to his face.

His eyebrow lifted, his fierce dark eyes shifted dangerously. "My name," he almost growled before dropping her hand like a red-hot branding iron.

Lacy rocked back on her heels. Goodness, where had all the air gone?

"Matlock Clint—I mean Clint Matlock, it's nice to m-meet you," she stammered. Wrapping her hands around her waist she lifted her shoulders, trying to act as if she had not just been poleaxed by his touch. "Now—" she cleared her throat "—do you have insurance?"

"Do *I* have insurance?" he asked, dropping his jaw. "What would I need insurance for?"

"Why, to pay for the damage to my Caddy."

A hoot of laughter rang out in the crowd Lacy had forgotten. Sheriff Brady chuckled. Clint glared at him, then peered down at Lacy.

Regaining her bravado, she smiled again making sure her dimples showed. "Since we're practically neighbors and all, I figured if you don't have insurance—I mean anyone who would drive a dusty old black Jeep—" She couldn't help teasing him. It covered up her nerves. She wagged her finger and clucked her tongue. "Well, you know how those sorts of people are…anyway, I'm certain we can come to an agreement if we just get creative. Besides, we don't want Sheriff Brady having to cuff us and throw us both into jail. Now do we?"

He stared at her, slack-jawed. It was a look Lacy had seen often on people she spoke to. A pin, or was it a needle, dropping into a haystack within a mile radius could have been heard. She waited patiently, enjoying that he was actually taking her seriously.

After a moment, a very long moment, he pulled his hat off his head, dropped his chin to his chest and studied his scuffed boots. Methodically, he slapped his Stetson against his thigh. His thick sandy hair fluttered in the humid breeze.

Lacy studied that mass of hair and waited. She knew she should come clean and confess that she'd only been joking. But he was so cute believing her. She was about to own up to her teasing just as Clint's shoulders shifted upward and a deep throaty laugh escaped him.

Lacy could only stare as Clint lifted his chin off his chest just high enough to cock his head to one side and slant those fabulous eyes her way.

"Are you here to catch a husband?" he asked softly.

"No!" She slapped a hand of denial over her heart so hard she choked. "No, I'm here to help everyone else find husbands."

He lifted his chin higher. He had a lean, square chin. A nice chin.

"And just how are you going to do that?"

"I'm going to style their hair."

"Their hair?" His lips slashed into a quizzical smile. "And that's going to make them fall in love?"

"Oh, yes. *Love is in the hair…*" she sang to the tune of the old *Love Boat* theme. Chortles and more hoots rippled through the crowd.

Clint rolled his eyes and strode to his injured Jeep.

"Clint," Brady called, watching him climb into the wreck. "What do you want me to do? She *is* new in town."

Clint slammed his hat back on his head before cranking his engine; grudgingly it coughed to life. "Let her go, Brady. I've got rustlers to catch, and if I stand here much longer, trying to figure out little Miss Lacy Brown, I'm afraid I'll get back to the ranch and my entire herd will be gone."

"If that's what you want," Brady said.

Lacy took a step toward the Jeep. Clint dropped the gear into reverse and rammed it into drive. Then settling his hat more snugly on his forehead, he guided the clanking heap in a sad lurching arch northward.

Watching him go, a dangerous sense of anticipation rippled through Lacy.

She did not like the feeling one bit.

Chapter Two

Standing on the side of the road, Clint peered at his Jeep's radiator. Steam boiled from it, tangling with the smoke curling from the engine. In his haste to get out of Dodge and away from Lacy Brown, he'd just driven off.

That walking tornado had wiped out his good sense. That would explain how he hadn't given a thought to the damage to his vehicle or that it might not make the ten-mile trip back to the ranch. Now, stranded on the side of the road, he had to be content to wait for a ride or walk the last four miles home. He still needed a cup of coffee, but it looked like today wasn't his day for one, or anything else.

He owned a cell phone, but little good that did him out here in the bowels of Texas without reception. It was the luck of the day that this long stretch between

Mule Hollow and the ranch was the deader than dead zone.

Outsmarted by a bunch of cattle thieves, then accosted by Lacy Brown, now this—what a combination. Of course, to be fair, he owed Ms. Brown an apology. It was his fault that he'd hit her car. No excuses, all that grief he'd given her about her insurance had been wrong. He shouldn't have carried it so far.

Clint couldn't help thinking that if *she* was what that advertisement Norma Sue and the ladies put out was bringing to town—Mule Hollow was in worse trouble than before the oil wells had dried up.

Rubbing the back of his neck, he walked to the center of the deserted farm-to-market road and stood there, boots planted on both sides of the yellow line. "Nothin' coming down this road anytime soon," he said to the birds gliding high in the blue sky above him.

His ranch and just a few other homes were all that were out this direction from town. This bit of road was as dead as town.

He started walking.

He hated what had happened to the town he'd grown up in. Like all the folks with roots dating back two and three generations, watching the town die had been a hard thing to stomach. Especially when he remembered what a pretty little place it had been before the oil boom busted in the late seventies. He'd only been a kid, but he remembered all the oil rigs that had once dotted the pastures along this countryside. When the wells dried up, the roughnecks took their families and moved on to find work somewhere else. Their departure left Mule Hollow just that—*hollow.*

Nowadays, most all the town had left were herds of cattle and lonesome cowboys.

And man alone didn't build a town.

Mule Hollow needed women in order to build families. But the town had nothing to offer ladies. Ranching was long hard work, which left little time for the men to travel over an hour to the nearest town to find a date. It wasn't happening.

That's when the few older women who were left had a revelation from the Lord Himself, as they put it, and they realized Mule Hollow did have a commodity.

Mule Hollow had men.

And that was the start of this harebrained plan and the advertisement for wives. An ad for wives! It sounded like a mail-order bride scheme right out of an old Western. But actually it was straight from Norma Sue Jenkins's family tree. Her great-great-grandma had been a real-life mail-order bride. And a success story to boot.

That didn't mean this would be. And if the women who might respond to that ad were anything like Lacy Brown, then Mule Hollow was probably better off remaining a dried-up hole-in-the-road. The woman really worried him. He'd seen women like her up close, too close. They didn't stay, they didn't stick. And women who didn't stick around when times were rough weren't worth having around in the first place.

Clint paused, took his hat off and wiped his forehead with the back of his hand. He'd reached the mesquite-and-wire fencing of his ranch boundaries. That meant he only had three more miles to go to the ranch house, a shower and that cup of coffee he'd never gotten.

Picking up his pace, his spurs clinking on the pavement, he let his thoughts dwell on the town's predicament rather than his own.

His men were excited about women coming. They were young and he was glad for them. But he himself had no intention of being *bait*. For all he cared, women could flock in by the thousands, but it wouldn't change his mind.

Like he'd said, he, Clint Matlock, had seen up close how fickle women could be, and he would never be one of the men who tried to make this town survive through the sharing of a bunch of useless vows.

Lacy shoved a pile of trash out of the way with the toe of her boot. Sheri had been griping ever since they'd entered the deplorable building. "Use your imagination, Sheri. Everything you see here is purely cosmetic, easily remedied. And *that* will give the salon super atmosphere."

"Yeah, right. Lace, it's a crumbling brick wall for goodness' sake."

Lacy studied the object of Sheri's horror. "It's upscale. Think like a New Yorker."

"In a place named Mule Hollow?" Sheri frowned and arched an eyebrow. "I don't think so."

Standing side by side, they studied the brick wall that ran the full length from store front to back. It was bad, but Lacy had seen worse. After her father had run out on them, Lacy and her mother had moved into their share of run-down apartments in the Dallas Metroplex. Lacy's mom, bless her soul, had never let Lacy know the despair she must have felt. Instead, she'd taught her daughter vision, to look beyond the grime and see the beauty that they could create as a team of two. And oh, what beauty they'd created... Thinking of those apartments, the wonder of a lot of elbow grease, discounted paint and tons of love, made Lacy smile. She and Sheri were each so lost in their observations that they didn't hear the footsteps behind them.

"Lacy is right, Sheri. You have to look past the rubbish and deterioration to see what can be."

Startled, Sheri and Lacy spun around to find three older ladies standing just inside the doorway beaming at them.

"Hello," said the smiling trio.

"Hello," said the young pair clutching their chests, hearts thumping.

These were the ladies of the town, the wise women who had dreamed the dream and followed through with a plan. Lacy was immediately drawn to them. She studied them warmly as introductions were made. There was Esther Mae Wilcox, with her flaming red hair piled high on her head like a triple dip of red velvet ice cream. She had beautiful smooth skin kissed by flecks of freckles. At first glance with the gigantic hair in the way, Esther looked a good ten years older than the early sixties Lacy figured her to be. She knew on sight that Esther Mae would be her first makeover.

Norma Sue Jenkins had the figure of a basketball, but oozed life from every pore of her sun-leathered skin. Her salt-and-pepper hair was as wiry as anything Lacy had seen in all her years behind the chair. That it could use a little conditioner was an understatement. Conditioner and a good cut, Lacy knew a woman in need of a little TLC when she saw one. And that just happened to be her specialty.

Then there was Adela Ledbetter. It was obvious she'd found a salon somewhere. Her snow-white hair had been cut into a stylish pixie. A wisp of bangs softened the look, highlighting the brightest, most intelligent sapphire eyes Lacy had ever seen. In this woman's eyes, Lacy saw a kindred spirit and the true dream of the town.

"You placed the ad," Lacy said, accepting Adela's proffered hand.

"Yes," she said. Her voice was gentle and cultured. It seemed completely out of place in a town like Mule Hollow.

"Against the wishes of the men," Norma Sue boomed, coming forward to grab both Lacy and Sheri's hands at the same time and pumping them enthusiastically.

"Men! What do they know anyway?" Esther Mae scowled and bobbed her triple-decker.

Lacy chuckled, grateful when Norma Sue let go of her hand. "I couldn't agree more. I gathered from a conversation with Sam that the guys aren't with the program?"

"Well, yes and no." Norma Sue sighed. "Some of them want to be, they really do. But they don't have the eyes to see the big picture. They don't trust the good Lord enough to know that He could work a miracle and keep our town alive."

"So, my good ladies, we have to show them that trust and faithfulness go hand in hand and lead to bountiful gifts," Adela said.

Esther patted her hair, nodding. "The fellas in this town won't know what hit them."

"Boy, is that an understatement," Sheri said. "I have to say, though, that I'm going to enjoy watching all the fireworks this plan ignites. Like earlier with Lacy and Clint. That poor guy didn't know what to do with her."

"He needed that shaking up," said Norma Sue. "The

way that boy works, you would think there is no tomorrow. He needs to get back right with God and find out there is more to life than work."

"I'm glad I came," Lacy said. "I think the plan you've hatched will be a great success. And Clint Matlock is the poster boy for this campaign even if he doesn't know it." She strode lightly to the window and stared out across the town. Following her gaze, the ladies moved to stand beside her. She wondered if they could see what she saw. "This is going to be a happening place within the next few weeks. We're going to make people fall in love, get married. Make babies. Y'all, we're going into the matchmaking business, but more, we're going into the business of futures." *And I'm going into the business of leading souls to Christ.*

All eyes turned to her.

Adela inclined her head to one side, her smile serious. "The first match could be you. Sam said the sparks were really flying between you and Clint. God could have brought you all this way to lead the way."

Sheri choked.

Lacy did likewise and stepped back from the expectant group. "No way! I'm here to run a business. I'll spruce these gals up so the men can't resist them and I'll help you do whatever I can to make this venture a success. But whatever you do, don't try matching me up with anyone."

"But the sparks—" Esther May said.

Lacy held up her hand to stop Esther's words. "Sparks or no sparks, I'm not in the market for a hubby."

"Well, for crying out loud, why not?" Norma Sue asked.

At the moment, Lacy didn't want to give her life story on the reasons men weren't at the top of her list. But serious relationships that led to marriage were out of the question for now. "I've got a business to build here. You've got a town to build. By mutual agreement, I think my energies would serve better if I weren't sidetracked by a man hunt of my own. I'm here to concentrate on God and His plan. Not mine."

"Well," Adela said, "I think that's an admirable mission. If we all put God first, just think where we'd be. And you're absolutely right about Clint Matlock. When the women get here and see him strutting down the sidewalk, fireworks are going to strike somebody."

"Which will be good to see." Esther Mae snorted. "The boy's been hard to understand ever since his mama ran off with the circus. He needs some good woman to come along and show him not all women are deserters."

The circus? Now that sounded interesting and sad. Lacy wrestled down her curiosity. There was no doubt sparks would fly any time that cowboy was around. But that was only because Clint Matlock was a big, grumpy ol' lump of coal.

* * *

Clint fought his growing frustration as he studied the deep tire ruts crossing the line between pastures on the back section of his ranch. The fence separating the land had been cut and another thirty head of cattle were gone. He'd taken heavy losses over the past three months and was at a standstill on how to catch the thieves. Ranches as expansive as his were hard to protect at all times.

His foreman, Roy Don Jenkins, stood beside him surveying the damage too. Removing his hat, he scratched the top of his gray head. "You thinkin' what I'm thinkin'?" he asked.

Clint curled his fingers around the dangling barbed wire. "That unless someone happens to run up on something they aren't supposed to see or the rustlers make a stupid mistake, we're straight out of luck."

"Yup, 'bout sums it up." Roy Don settled his hat back on his head and spat a long stream of tobacco.

Clint pulled his leather gloves from his back pocket and yanked them on. He had hired hands who could repair the cut fence, but he needed the exertion. He'd been restless since going into town yesterday, and he'd learned early on from his father that work always helped a man through a restless time. Mac Matlock had been a hardworking man. He'd built his life from the land and the cattle that grazed on it. He'd instilled that same sense of commitment into Clint. After Clint's mama left them, Clint had learned from watching his dad that a man could get through anything working out alone on the open range.

Reaching for his tools, Clint prepared to fix the fence. He was preoccupied with finding a way to catch the rustlers at their game.

Roy Don spat another stream of tobacco then grasped a section of wire, as always, ready to help. "Norma Sue can't quit talkin' 'bout the new beauty operator. Says she's a real go-getter."

Clint shook his head. "You saw my Jeep."

Roy Don laughed. "Yup. While I was down at Pete's picking up feed, I heard about all that business yesterday morning. Funny you didn't mention it."

"Well, I'm glad to be the entertainment for the boys at the feed store. Didn't mention it 'cause it wasn't important."

"It sounded like you had your hands full."

Clint lifted his gaze and met the older man's. "You should have seen her, Roy Don. She looked like a feisty hen protecting her chicks, puffing out her chest and standing me off." Thinking about those sparkling, denim-colored eyes flashing at him… *Oh, no, you don't.* The last thing he wanted to do was talk about Lacy Brown.

He wanted to forget her. She had distracted him enough.

Roy Don spat and kept on talking. "Come out here

five hundred miles from Dallas. Drove it all in one night. Sam said that friend of hers told him, once Lacy Brown got an idea in her head, there was no stoppin' her. Said God gave her a vision about Mule Hollow. You think God really speaks out like that nowadays? Gal's got guts, up and moving here like she did."

That, or she was just plain crazy. Why else would she load up and move to a strange town? Clint was of the opinion that anyone who'd drive that awful pink convertible had to be a tad soft in the brains. But he kept his mouth shut and cranked on the wire stretcher in the hopes that his foreman might get the idea and get back to work.

He didn't.

"Norma Sue said she was more excited about this crazy scheme of theirs than they were. Said, she, Adela and Esther had been a bit worried until they talked to Lacy." He paused, thoughtfully twisting the tip of his mustache. "I don't know Clint, but I'm of a mind to think this could get pretty entertaining."

Clint snorted. Finished with the fence he stripped off his gloves and strode toward his truck. "Roy Don," he said, tossing the wire stretcher into the bed of the truck, "things could also get out of hand. Lacy Brown looked like trouble to me. Trouble with a capital *T*."

Chapter Three

On her third morning in Mule Hollow, Lacy decided to get her routine started right away. The sun was just waking up again and the dew was thick on the grass. Standing on the front porch of the cute frame house Norma Sue had arranged for them to rent, Lacy slowly went through her stretches preparing for her morning jog. The house was in the country down a dirt road all by itself, surrounded by endless green pastures. Birds were twittering and bees were humming around a wonderfully fragrant honeysuckle vine that wove around a post at the corner of the yard. The place was lovely.

Pausing in her stretch, Lacy bowed her head in prayer. *Thank you, Lord, for bringing me to this wonderful town. You know my heart and I pray that You will use me for Your glory. But once more I pray let this be about You and not about me. Teach me patience and meekness…put tape on my mouth if You have to. Let Your will be done. Amen.*

Energy filled Lacy as she jogged down the dirt road. She'd already started exploring the town last night in her own special way—midnight cruises in her convertible. There was nothing better than a late-night drive. But now, she had this quiet dirt road just outside her door perfect for jogging and meditating.

Looking up, she was filled with more peace as the trees laced their branches into a canopy above her and sunlight filtered through in bright shafts of light leading a pathway along the road. A few more feet and she burst from the trees and into a section where cattle-speckled pasture land was separated from the road by thin wire. A few lifted their heads as she passed them, then returned to breakfast.

She hadn't gone too far when the most pitiful wail she'd ever heard jolted her from her thoughts. She stopped running and scanned the surrounding land for the site of the terrible sound, "Maww". It came again just as she spotted a tiny, white-faced calf struggling in the grass. It was in obvious distress as it fought to get up. The mother cow paced back and forth behind the calf, no less upset. Lacy moved to the fence, unsure how to handle the situation, but knowing she couldn't keep going without doing something. The cow cried out mournfully. It was such hopeless sound. Lacy climbed through the wire fence before she could stop herself.

She didn't have the vaguest idea of what to do, but she was the only person around. She couldn't pass on by.

As she approached, Mama Cow turned fearful eyes toward her. Pushing away her own fear, Lacy eased farther into the pasture, leaving behind the safety of the fence. "Relax, pretty lady. I just want to see what's wrong with your sweet baby. Her crying is making my heart ache."

As if to say hurry, the baby cried louder and its mama grew more agitated, swinging her head from side to side. At close range Lacy was surprised at how tiny the calf was. She didn't know much about cows and things, but this poor baby couldn't be too old, maybe a few days, or even just a few hours old. What she did know was that it was very weak. Its hoof was caught between two small tree stumps and ants were crawling all over it.

"Oh, you poor baby," Lacy gasped. Time was of the essence. Everyone knew that in Texas you didn't mess around with fire ants. They would kill the calf if she didn't act quickly. Keeping one eye on the babe, she yanked her sweatshirt off, thankful she'd worn it and a tank top to jog in today because she needed something to dust the ants off the baby. As she edged toward the calf the mama snorted and lowered her head. Lacy had seen bull riding on television, and if her hunches were right, this was probably a universal stance of war among all cattle breeds.

"Whoa there, girl. I've risked my life with your mama cow over there, the least you can do is give a girl a chance." Lacy prayed Mama wouldn't charge with her baby between them, so she quickly moved behind the crying calf.

Not wasting any time, she swatted the calf. This startled the calf, who bellowed in terror, causing Mama to paw the earth angrily. Lacy did not like the look gleaming in her deceptively calm eyes and dusted harder and faster. Mama stepped forward. Growing anxious Lacy grasped the calf's leg then, trying to be careful, she yanked it free, lost her balance and she and the baby tumbled backward. When she hit the ground she found herself lying with the baby sprawled on top of her.

Not thinking about protection, she gently pushed the babe off of her and stood. "You are a heavy little fella," she said, not liking the pain in the little guy's eyes. Bending forward, she gently rubbed him between his huge brown eyes then ran her hands down his body flicking off the last of the ants.

From behind her she heard a very angry snort.

Lacy's heart slammed into her throat. Spinning around she found herself facing a furious mama cow, who was glaring at her. The mixed up mama was pawing the ground and thrashing her head from side to side. Uneasy, Lacy stepped back, glancing around the pasture, she searched for an escape.

Then, mad-cow-Mama charged!

* * *

Clint urged his horse forward as he neared the front pasture. It was a still, quiet morning that promised to be another scorching Texas day in July. Heat simmered about him, causing a thin film of perspiration to bead across his brow. It was his kind of morning.

He respected everything there was about the way God had created summer in Texas. If ridden right you had no problems, ridden wrong you suffered consequences. He'd learned at an early age to work while the day was young, take your time while the sun was high and finish your chores as the sun moved west. This morning he was looking for a missing pregnant heifer due to drop her calf at any time. He wanted to move her closer to the house, so he could help with the delivery if needed. Clint enjoyed the birthing process; it made him smile.

And those didn't come easy to Clint.

Approaching the tree line separating the two pastures, he was alarmed when a shrieking scream filled the calm morning air. By the mere flick of his heel Clint sent his horse galloping through the pine trees just in time to see a tiny woman sprinting across his pasture. An angry cow was right on her tail.

Now, seeing a woman racing about his land wasn't a normal everyday sight. However, when he realized it was Lacy Brown burning rubber in his pasture, he wasn't surprised. Nothing this woman could do would shock Clint.

His horse, always ready for a chase, easily cleared the fence and took up pursuit of the two ladies. Like lightning and thunder, they were close together, striking out toward a lone tree in the center of the clearing.

"Get behind the tree," he yelled, even though he didn't think Lacy Brown in her obvious terror could hear him.

And then, just when he thought she would be trampled, Lacy took a flying leap, grasped a tree limb and swung effortlessly up into the tree branches.

Clint pulled his horse to an abrupt halt, disbelieving what he'd just witnessed. He pushed his hat back on his forehead and scratched his temple. That tree limb looked to be about seven feet off the ground. Her athletic lunge had looked like that of a seasoned acrobat.

"Whew, that was close," she gasped from above, clearly out of breath.

As he stared in bewildered silence, she pushed a branch out of her way and peered out at him.

"Am I glad you showed up," she panted. "I thought I was done for. Can you do anything with that cow?"

Clint pushed his hat back farther. "That depends, Miss Brown, on what *you* are doing here in my pasture at the crack of dawn?"

"Your pasture? I thought this belonged to Norma Sue's boss." Her eyes widened and she shifted on her perch.

"I am Norma Sue's boss."

"Oh, my…" She moved a branch farther out of her way. "Then you're my landlord."

"Your what?"

"Landlord. Norma Sue rented us that small house up by the road."

"You're joking. Right?" Clint felt a severe sinking sensation in his gut. His saddle groaned loudly as he shifted uneasily.

"Nope. Wouldn't joke at a time like this." Her brow furrowed as she looked from him to the heifer, now standing contently to one side of the tree. "Why isn't that cow chasing you?"

"Oh, her, that's Flossy. She wouldn't hurt a fly."

"Ha! She almost killed me."

"All you had to do was turn around and flap your arms at her." Her look of frustration gave Clint an odd sense of satisfaction after the way she'd mouthed off the morning before.

"No way. That cow wanted my blood."

"Nope." He shook his head, loving her distress. "I assure you, you can get down now."

"Not on your life, bud. That cow is crazy."

"Look who's calling the kettle black." Clint dismounted and went to stand beneath her.

"You are saying that with a smile on your face. I hope."

His lips twitched. "A small one, but it's there."

"Well, good. I'd hate to have to fall out of this tree and belt you one."

Clint removed his hat, ran a hand through his hair. "Did your mama ever tell you what a handful you are?"

"All the time. Now about my playing monkey—"

"You don't have to keep hanging around up there. Flossy isn't going to hurt you and I need to go and find her baby."

"Her baby! Ants were attacking the poor thing." She started to drop down and stopped. "You are certain Flossy isn't coming after me again?"

"Certain." Clint sighed, holding out his arms. "Come on down. I'll help you."

"No, thanks. I can handle this."

She slipped from the tree, dropping to her feet in front of him. She had on plain gray athletic pants, and a lime-green top with no sleeves. She had lovely arms, tanned and lean. Even a mess, Lacy Brown was a sight to behold.

Flossy snorted and Lacy sprang up against him. Before he could snag his good sense, he wrapped his arms around her...all for the sake of protection. She fit in his arms like she'd been made to be there. It was a very pleasant feeling. Her wispy hair tickled his nose, tempting him with the inviting scent of lemons. He loved the smell of lemons— "Come on," he growled. Lacy looked up at him and blinked. She had a set of very deceptive eyes. They seemed almost innocent. He had a hard time believing this could be true of such a wildfire of a woman. He dropped his arms and stepped away. "Flossy isn't going to harm you."

"If you say so." She stepped away from him. "But I'll walk on this side of you just in case." She quickly sidestepped around him, placing him beside Flossy.

Clint fought the need to smile.

"The calf is over here," she said, and started trotting.

Clint fell in beside her. The spitfire had a tender heart.

They jogged a few yards before he saw the calf.

"He was crying terribly when I came around the corner. It scared me to death at first. I never knew something so small could make a noise like that. It was heartbreaking. I couldn't stand it if he died."

They reached the tiny babe together and Clint dropped to his knees. Lacy plunked down and gently took the little fella's head into her lap. He hadn't moved and was breathing heavily.

"Tell me he's going to be all right."

He was covered in bites, but Clint had seen worse. Nevertheless, it was obvious that if Lacy hadn't intervened, the ants would have killed the calf. "He'll make it. Thanks to you. I owe you."

Lacy just nodded. When she looked up at him there were tears in her eyes.

No, not tears— He lifted the calf in his arms, fighting to ignore the way his heart was thumping. Lacy stood, too, then walked over and picked up a red sweatshirt.

"Is that what you beat the ants off him with?"

She nodded and after inspecting it for more ants, she yanked it over her head then pushed the arms up to her elbows.

"That was quick thinking on your part. Thanks again," he said.

Returning to his side Lacy gently rubbed the curly white forehead of the weak baby. "You're welcome. I couldn't stand the thought of him dying." The wind whipped at her pale hair and Clint had another crazy urge. He wanted suddenly to tuck the feathery strands behind her ear and kiss away the worry lines creased between her eyebrows. Whoa, Clint…you're one sadistic fool! What'd he think he'd do with a woman like Lacy Brown? She'd be the kind of woman who'd bring a man to his knees, wild, unpredictable—and then when he couldn't think straight anymore, she'd be the kind to walk away. And never look back.

"The calf will be fine," he snapped, trying to ignore how cute her quizzical expression was.

"Did I say something wrong?"

"Nope."

She dropped her hand and stepped back. "You're sure. You look like you just ate a lemon."

Lemons— "Nothing is wrong, I need to get going is all."

"Can I help?"

"No!"

Her lovely eyebrows shot together. "There is something wrong. The calf is sicker than you're telling me."

She stepped closer. Her bare forearm brushed his and he froze. Sweat popped across his forehead when she lifted her gaze to his. Lacy Brown's eyes were bottomless pools of sapphire. They reminded him of pictures on a brochure he'd seen of the blue waters off the coast of Mexico. The travel brochure had boasted that you could see thirty feet deep in the crystal-clear water. It couldn't compare to the depths of Lacy's eyes.

"Clint, is the baby dying?"

"No—"

"Then I'll come by later to check on him."

"That won't be necessary."

"Yes, it will." She started to move toward the fence then stopped. "Flossy isn't going to trample me, is she?"

"She'll stick with her calf. Go on." Please.

"Well, if you say so." She eyed the cow warily before loping toward the road.

"Sorry about all this," he called stupidly, watching how she moved, liking her fluid movement. Enjoying what he saw way too much.

"No problem," she called over her shoulder. "I'm

glad to see all those years of gymnastics finally came in handy." She climbed through the fence then stopped. "See you later, neighbor." She waved high above her head.

He couldn't move as he watched her disappear around the bend in the road. Only after she was gone did he expel the breath that had stuck in his lungs.

"Not if I see you first," he muttered.

What could provoke those eyes to playfulness? The question hit Lacy like a sledgehammer. Oh, no, you don't, she thought, snapping from insane daydreams of Clint Matlock and back to her driving. She and Sheri were headed toward town to work on the salon.

"So he rescued you on his horse."

"No, Sheri."

"How romantic," Sheri sighed, ignoring Lacy's denial.

"There was nothing romantic about it. I almost got trampled by a ballistic cow."

"You know you enjoyed it."

"No, I did not enjoy the mad cow."

"You know perfectly well I'm talking about Clint Matlock with the dreamy dark eyes."

That was it. "Sheri, you know I'm not here to look for a guy."

"And why not?" Sheri turned to face Lacy.

"Because I don't have time. That's not part of the plan."

"That's a cop-out and you know it, Lacy Brown. God has someone out there for you and you can't pick the time and place for His plans to come together."

"Believe me, Sheri, Clint Matlock is not the man God has waiting for me. Why, we'd never have any peace if that were so. We'd be fighting all the time. And besides, I'm not ready."

Sheri sighed and relaxed into the seat. "When will you be ready? It's been a year since Dillon."

Dillon. Lacy tried not to think about him. Things had gotten better since her and Dillon's breakup, but it still hurt to think about Dillon's deception. She'd broken off their engagement when she'd realized that their life goals and faith were at odds with each other. She'd been determined to seek God's total will in her life even if it meant sacrifice on her part.

Still, Dillon's quick marriage not three months later had shocked and hurt. It stung her ego that he could move on so quickly. "I don't know when I'll be ready, Sheri. I just know I'm not ready right now."

Lacy learned three things immediately: the diner had good food; the jukebox really did only play "Great Balls of Fire" and if plans were to be made, they were thought up over coffee at Sam's Diner.

"Norma Sue, you've got to work on that music box," Esther Mae clucked as she scooted into the booth's bench across the table from Lacy.

Lacy watched Esther's hair and thought for a minute that the thing might topple off her head. She even wondered if the triple-decker might be a wig. But then, after close inspection, she decided the diabolical-do was all Esther Mae's.

"Now, Esther, hold on," Norma snapped. "You know I can fix small appliances." She nodded toward the jukebox. "Does that there music box look like a toaster?"

"I don't understand why if you can fix my toaster you can't figure out why *only* that one song plays on that machine."

"Esther Mae," Adela interjected calmly, "Norma Sue said she can't fix the jukebox. If she says she can't, then she can't. You'll simply have to learn to tune the music out."

"Tune it out. Goodness gracious!" Esther shrilled along with Jerry Lee. "It's kind of hard to tune out!"

"Sorry, Esther Mae," Lacy laughed. "I couldn't help plugging another nickel into the jukebox. I love it!"

Norma Sue eyed the jukebox like it had issued a personal challenge. "Sam, I'll be back tomorrow to work that thing over. If more new folks come to town, they'll be wanting to play it, too. So it needs to work, or it'll drive us crazy."

Lacy caught the small smile on Adela's lips. The little lady knew exactly what to say to get the job done.

"Thank ya, Norm. I appreciate the help. I got a toaster out back that needs fixing while you're here."

"Yeah, yeah," Norma Sue said, shaking her head.

"What's the deal with the toasters?" Sheri asked, thumping two sugar packets together.

Lacy would have asked, had she not been watching Sam curiously.

Everything paused as he placed a china cup full of creamy coffee in front of Adela and then asked for orders. It was interesting to Lacy that Adela hadn't asked for the coffee and also interesting that instead of the commercial ceramic mug everyone else in the place seemed to drink from, she received a dainty china cup. Also interesting was the plum color Sam turned when Adela smiled up at him in thanks. And although Lacy marked the scene in her memory as a point to ponder, no one else seemed the least bit surprised as they gave Sam their order.

As soon as he moved away, Sheri hunched over the table on her elbows and said, "Tell the tale about the toasters."

Norma sighed. "It's a long boring story. But I'll make it short. I can fix the things and I never get any peace because of it."

"So are you the town handyman?" Sheri asked.

"Woman," Norma corrected with a snort. "Sadly for me, I can fix anything as long as its insides are similar to a toaster."

"Once," Esther Mae piped in, "this fellow wanted to marry her because he thought she could fix his tractors. Norma Sue set him straight right quick. She was so mad she got up under all three of his tractors and messed them up. When she finished, he had parts lying everywhere."

"That-a-way Norma," Lacy said. Taking the soda Sam handed her, she saluted Norma.

Everyone followed by lifting their drinks, too. "Now I know who to call if something breaks in the salon. However, before you dismantle anything, simply tell me whether it's repairable or not. Or if I've angered you in any way that day."

Adela hid her mouth when Sam started laughing. "Yeah, poor Artie Holboney never did get those tractors working after that. Ended up he had to marry a woman in the junk business."

"Oh, Sam," Adela said, giving him a soft push on the arm. "He did no such thing."

Sam looked at her hand still resting on his arm and beamed like a rooster in a henhouse.

Lacy took in the blush that colored Adela's cheeks when she realized what Sam was looking at. Quickly she folded her hands in her lap. Lacy found the prospect of a blossoming romance between these two lovely people extremely motivating.

"Okay, girls, I think it's time to get down to business," she said. "Let's talk turkey about how to entice women to Mule Hollow. I need you to tell me your plans."

"Well," Esther Mae began, high-pitched and shrill. "There's a bunch of single teachers who teach at the community school we share with a few other small towns."

"Yeah," Norma Sue added. "We bus the few children who live here to a school twenty miles away. The teachers commute farther than that, because most of them live in Ranger, only because it has things to offer them."

Esther Mae nodded vigorously in agreement. Lacy watched her flaming dipper threatening to slide right off her head and do a swan dive off her nose into Norma's coffee.

"Things we don't have," Esther gushed. "Like beauty parlors and dress stores. And *aerodynamic* fitness centers!"

"Aerobic," Norma Sue shot at her. "Aerobic. They're not airplanes, for crying out loud."

"Whatever," Esther Mae quipped. "Anyway, where was I before I was so rudely interrupted? Oh, yes. We're remodeling the old Howard house across the street as a small apartment building. Adela, bless her heart, has the funds and wants to do this for the good of the town. Also, we thought we'd do a fair. You know, a street fair like we used to have years ago."

"Yup, used to have those fairs in our courting days," Norma Sue added. "Met my Roy Don at one. He could stack more hay bales faster than anyone. I kissed him when I gave him his trophy. Boy-hidie, that kiss sparked a lifetime of love so rich I still get teary-eyed thinking about it."

"Norma Sue," Esther Mae sighed, "Hank Wilcox ain't no slouch, either."

"Ladies," Adela added softly, "we aren't here to discuss your sweeties' attributes. Although I'm certain that they are wonderful. We're here to make some plans for the rest of the world to fall in love."

"Of course we are," Esther Mae agreed, smiling at Lacy. "Lacy, do you have any suggestions?"

She had been enjoying herself immensely and now Lacy hunched over the table conspiratorially, ever so ready to share her ideas. "I thought you'd never ask...."

Chapter Four

"Women! Clint, I just don't know what we're goin-t-do," Roy Don muttered, tugging at his fat gray mustache. He was pacing back and forth across Clint's office, the clink of his spurs punctuating each hard step. "I just don't know."

It had been another long night for Clint, staked out on the back side of the ranch watching for rustlers. Judging by Roy Don's agitated state, the day promised to be even longer. It was midmorning, and another scorcher. The sun had come up fighting mad, bringing Clint home from his stakeout sticky, stinking and wanting nothing more than a cool shower, a fresh cup of coffee and a positive report from his men, who had been camped out at other strategic points of the ranch.

What he'd gotten was Roy Don, pacing anxiously back and forth across his office. "Don't get me wrong," he was saying. "I, for one, couldn't live without my Norma Sue, but, Clint…this scheme of theirs is out of control."

"Relax, Roy Don. You know Norma Sue will settle down after a while. I figure, if any women come at all, it'll just be a few. If more show up…" He shrugged. "Who knows—maybe this *is* the way to revive Mule Hollow." Clint scratched his chest and eased toward the door and the shower.

"But, son, you don't understand. That's what I been tryin' to tell you. You ain't been to town in three days. You ain't seen what I saw this mornin'."

Since finding a trailblazing Lacy in his pasture, it was true Clint hadn't been into town. He'd been busy—with rustlers and all. It had absolutely nothing to do with her. "Roy Don, weren't you telling me just the other day that having her here could be fun?"

The older man's face sagged and he stopped pacing. "That was before. Before she got this all-fired idea of hers."

Clint scrubbed his stubby face; he was tired and he didn't just want that shower, he *needed* it. But his curiosity got the better of him. "What did she do? Tell me."

Roy Don shook his head. "I can't. I can't say the words. But—the town will never…and I mean *ever* be the same."

"Man, what's come over you? Rustlers don't even get under your skin like this."

"All I can say is go to town, Clint. See for yourself. Sam and Pete tried to get Hank Wilcox and me to talk to Esther Mae and Norma Sue. They told us to ask 'em to get *her* to reconsider! But naw, Hank and me figured them crazy women would come to their senses on their own and talk her out of it." He paused to suck in a long breath. He looked as if he'd been to his best friend's funeral. "We were wrong. Dead wrong."

Suddenly Clint was worried. "Roy Don, tell me what that woman's done. Tell me right this minute—"

"Nope. I had to come up on it by surprise—'bout near had a wreck, too. Son, you need the full impact." Slapping his hat against his thigh, he turned and strode toward the door. "It ain't right, Clint," he added tiredly. "It just ain't right."

That was all Clint needed. He snatched his hat from the rack and was in his truck speeding down the road within seconds. Toward what, he didn't know. Roy Don was the mildest-mannered man he'd ever met. It baffled him, wondering what Lacy Brown had done. What could be awful enough to upset the man so much?

A quarter of a mile before Mule Hollow, he nearly drove into the ditch when the town's outline appeared on the horizon. No, way, she wouldn't! Clint cringed, squinting into the distance.

Sure as the day was bright, she was painting her two-story plank building *pink!*

Not just any pink. Hot pink. The fluorescent color used to paint steps. The kind intended to keep people from breaking their necks—ha! Fat chance. He could already see the pileups. The broken bones. The jokes.

Roy Don had been right. This couldn't happen. What had the women been thinking?

Soon as he brought his truck to a screeching halt in front of the atrocious offense, he slammed out of it, asking, "What in thunder do you think you're doing?"

From the rungs of her ten-foot ladder, she stared down at him. He was ready for war, but he had a sinking feeling when his eyeballs suddenly glued themselves to the sight of her in a pair of bleached-out cutoff blue jeans.

"Pretty in Pink."

Lacy's amused voice broke through the fog. "What?" he managed. Pushing his Stetson back from his forehead with his thumb, his eyes moved up and found her smiling radiantly at him. She was beautiful.

"'Pretty in Pink.' It's the name of the paint. Don't you like it?"

Like it. Clint tried unsuccessfully to focus on her words. Pale as a full moon, her hair spiked out from beneath a bright yellow baseball cap that proclaimed Bad Hair Day across the front. And it wasn't lying, but did that stop him from having the urge to pull off the cap?

"Woman." He bit the word out, angry at himself.

"You do like making a spectacle of yourself, don't you?"

"And what does that mean?" She continued to stare down at him.

"The way I figure it, when a woman shows off that much flesh, she's begging to be looked at." What are you doing, Matlock?

She plopped one paintbrush-wielding hand on her hip and a spray of pink paint showered down on him.

"Hey, look out."

"I'll have you know it's a hundred degrees out here. If a man were painting this building, he'd be shirtless. Like I said the other day, you have some issues with being kind of a chauvinistic snob."

"I most certainly do not," he denied, slapping his hand on the side of the ladder.

"Hey, watch out," she scolded when the ladder shifted. "Far be it from me to ruin your fantasy, if you can't face the truth."

Clint stiffened. "Look who's talking—a woman painting a place of business the color of…of lipstick."

"I'll have you know, a loud color will attract attention."

"What kind of attention? That's all I'm asking. I thought you were here to curl hair. Looks like you're here to curl some fella's toes."

"Clint Matlock. The pink is so everyone will know my salon on sight. Also, it'll get a little talk going. Draw a bit of attention."

"That's what I said." Clint scanned the street. Everyone in town, what few there were at this time of day, either stood on the street corner watching, or peered out a window. Across the street at the feed store, a few of the boys leaned against the porch enjoying the show. He wondered why none of them had offered to help. But then, why interfere? This scheme the ladies had cooked up wouldn't work. Guilt hit Clint. She was, in her weird way, trying to help all these guys.

Softening his tone he asked, "How long have you been at this?"

She'd resumed painting and her hips swayed gently to the rhythm of the brush.

"Since sunup."

"Five hours?"

"Yup." She stretched and painted as high as she could reach and still didn't get the last five feet of the building.

"It's time for a break."

"What?" She straightened, latching her gaze to his.

"I said it's time you climbed down from that stage and moved your body into the shade for a while. You'll have a heatstroke up there."

Big blue innocent eyes blinked down at him. "Look, Clint," she said, as she resumed painting, "I have a building to paint before tomorrow."

"Lacy." Clint slapped a rung of the ladder again to get her attention; she really did need to get out of the sizzling sun before she had a heatstroke. In his exasperation, he slapped the ladder too hard and it shifted.

"Ohhh…" she cried as the thing started sliding. "Ohhh—ohhh—"

Unable to believe what he'd done, Clint scrambled to stop the runaway ladder from falling. He grasped at the rungs, missed and caught Lacy's ankle instead.

Clinging to the ladder, she yelped when it twisted around and put Clint in front of the ladder staring up at a wobbling can of paint! He knew he was in trouble, but he held on to her ankle. He had gotten Lacy into this mess and he would get her out of it. It seemed for a moment that time stopped. One second she was clinging to the ladder, the paint can balanced before her, and then she was dropping into his arms. Unfortunately, the paint landed first.

Her eyes were huge saucers. Her chest heaved and for the briefest moment her sassy veneer disappeared, making her seem almost vulnerable. Clint felt a surprising and overwhelming compulsion to protect her, as she had protected the helpless calf.

She blinked, her eyes narrowed and the helpless aura vanished. "Is it just me, or do you accost all the new residents of Mule Hollow?"

And he'd just associated her with the word *helpless*. "Who's attacking who?" he asked drolly. "I'm the one with the pink paint dripping off my eyebrows."

Her lip quivered. "And I must say it's a fine color for

you. But if you hadn't thrown a hissy and smacked my ladder, I'd still be painting and you'd be your same dry self."

Frowning, he set her away from him, pivoted on his heel and headed toward his truck.

"See what I mean," she called.

He glanced over his shoulder. She stood hipshot and smiling, looking better than he looked at this moment.

"Temper, temper," she clucked.

"Should have dropped you," he muttered then climbed into his truck and hightailed it away from her.

Lacy watched Clint's black truck disappearing into the heat, fumes radiating off the long stretch of pavement. That man really got under her skin. And she meant *really*. Why, she had goose bumps, thinking about how she'd felt being held in his arms. Twice she'd been there and twice she'd liked it. But oh, how she didn't want to.

"You know he makes you all gooey inside," Sheri said, coming to stand beside her.

Lacy quirked an eyebrow and frowned.

Sheri didn't take the hint. "Don't give me that look. You know you're not dead inside that hyperactive skin of yours. You know Clint Matlock is tempting. Admit it."

Lacy couldn't help it. She smiled. "Okay, the guy is…interesting."

"Ha! Interesting. Lacy Brown, you know good and well that if male magnetism could be copied and sold it'd be Clint Matlock they'd be using."

"Really, Sheri, I'd think you have a crush on the man."

"It's not me he can't keep his eyes off."

Lacy whirled away and started toward the alley, where the water hose was connected to the hydrant. Sure, she liked what she saw. She was curious, too. About a lot of things, like why the man was so controlling. Did it have anything to do with his mom running away with the circus? And had he ever overcome the pain rejection like that caused a kid to harbor? And what had that done to his faith?

She pushed aside old feelings of betrayal as they swept over her. She'd had her own feelings to overcome when her father had walked out on her and her mom. Only through the love of her heavenly Father had she been able to forgive her birth father. Still, sometimes the raw ache would slip back in and she questioned why. She was human; abandonment left scars.

"You can't keep bringing this up, Sheri. It's not time for me to think about this. I don't want to think about it."

Sheri was leaning against the wall watching her. Lacy turned on the water hose and sprayed herself, clothes and all.

"When is a good time?"

"When I say."

"Lacy, Dillon was a jerk. I'd say more but my mom taught me better."

"This isn't about Dillon, or my father, for that matter. How many times must we go through this? This is about me and what I've committed to do for the Lord. I'm here to learn to put Christ first and me second. That goes for relationships, too. Dillon wasn't a Christian." Lacy halted her words when Sheri started shaking her head. Lacy jutted out her chin and frowned. Why did Sheri keep doing this? "I know he misled me—"

"Misled you! Lacy, the guy lied to you. He willingly caused you to believe he was committed to God. He knew what you were looking for in a man, so he faked being what you wanted."

Reluctantly Lacy thought back to the painful memory, then forced it aside. "That's beside the point. God had a plan for me, period. He is in control and this is where I was supposed to come. I'm grateful that things didn't work out between me and Dillon. Really I am." Finishing up with the water Lacy walked over and turned off the faucet. "I believe with all my heart that this is where God intended me to be…building a business. Not, and may I repeat, not finding a man!"

"That's all very good, Lacy. But like I keep telling you, you can't pick the time, place or who you're going to fall in love with. I just don't think you need to fight this obvious attraction with Clint. He could be the one."

Lacy sighed long and hard and counted to ten. What was she going to do with Sheri? "Okay, let's think about this differently. What, please tell me, has given you that idea? If you think about it, Clint and I haven't spoken more than about six civil sentences. That hardly constitutes the basis for a loving, Christian relationship."

Sheri smiled. "Sometimes people around you can see what you don't want to see. And believe me, I see plenty."

Lacy pulled off her cap and ran a restless hand through her curls. "I don't even know if Clint has a relationship with Christ. Believe me, I'm not making any more mistakes, Sheri. I'll pray long and hard about the next man I fall in love with and I'll make certain to see some fruit from his Christian walk before I say I do."

Sheri nodded. "I guess you're right about that. But I bet Clint is going to pass muster."

"And that would be wonderful if he did. But right now it's back to work. Do you see how much of that building I still have to paint."

Roy Don came out of the office as Clint was stalking stiff-legged toward the house. Since paint was drying in places he didn't care to scrub with a wire brush, Clint didn't stop to explain. Instead he held up a hand.

"Don't say anything. Not one word. It's not a pretty story. You can get one of the boys to clean up my truck seat."

A smart man, Roy Don knew when to hide a grin. "It's as good as taken care of."

Clint stamped to the house and yanked open the back door. At long last he was finally getting the shower he'd been dreaming of all night, while hiding in the bushes waiting on rustlers, and he couldn't even enjoy it for all the scrubbing he was going to have to endure.

Twenty minutes later, scrubbed nearly raw, his skin now pinker than any paint Lacy Brown could possibly concoct, Clint stood before the mirror in his bathroom and studied his hair with dismay. He'd already dressed in loose jeans and a navy polo shirt before he'd looked at himself in the mirror and realized that not all the paint had been destroyed.

Lacy Brown had painted his hair pink!

He looked like a lead guitarist for one of those hard-rock bands. Letting out a groan, he planted his palms on either side of the sink and leaned toward the mirror. He was up a creek without a paddle. If just one of his ranch hands saw this, he'd never live down the joking. Texas cowboys delighted in a chance to poke fun at some poor sodbuster. The boss drew the jokes ten-fold if he happened to be the one caught in a tender situation. Pink hair! Not in a million years would he have ever thought something like this could happen to him. Of course, since Lacy had come to town, there had been a lot happening to him that he'd never have dreamed of. But this—he'd have to find a way to get rid of the stuff. Pronto.

Lacy would know how.

The thought slipped into his thoughts, but he quickly put it away; he wasn't about to ask her. Not after the way he'd treated her. *Yeah, how have you treated her?* He stared at himself as he lathered on shaving cream, then wiped his hands on a towel. The woman had come to town to open a business and, in her spastic mind, help the town. She might have her own motives about being here, but essentially, from the little he'd been able to understand from her, she had noble ideas about helping Mule Hollow survive. He ran a hand through his hair and smiled remembering the way she'd suddenly started singing right there in the middle of town after they'd had their little driving mishap. The woman was—he hated to say it—the woman was *sometimes* entertaining and beautiful in a Meg Ryan sort of way. She did have a way of making him smile….

And she was out in that hot sun painting all alone because not a soul had offered to help.

He ignored the pang of guilt; instead he picked up his razor and started to shave his face while trying not to look himself in the eye. So what if it was a hundred degrees outside? Could he help it if the crazed woman didn't know when to quit? He wasn't her keeper—he met his gaze in the mirror. Somebody needed to be!

Chapter Five

Sweat trickled down Lacy's face so she paused her painting, pulled off her cap and wiped the bucket of perspiration from her forehead with the back of her arm. It was blazing hot. Clint had been right about that. She hated to admit it, but maybe she should get out of the sun and rest. She didn't have time, though. Why she'd only painted a little bit of her building and she wanted a whole lot more accomplished before she stopped. She hadn't even stopped to eat. There was so much to be done. Sheri needed help inside. The walls and woodwork needed painting, wallpaper had to be hung…the list went on and on.

Help would be nice, but Adela and the girls were busy overseeing the remodeling of the old Howard place. They needed some sort of accommodation for the women when they did come, and someone had to take care of that. Lacy understood and agreed that the apartments were a wonderful idea. Besides, it was too hot out here for them.

Dizziness swept over her; she swayed. For support, she grasped the railing that ran the length of the second-story roof. After a moment, the woozy feeling diminished and she placed her brush on the side of the paint bucket. Maybe going in wasn't such a bad idea…just for a minute anyway. She scanned the horizon, took a deep breath of sultry air and started to climb down from her perch on top of the front overhang, when three trucks materialized out of the distant road haze.

Clicking along at a fast pace, they looked like they were on a mission. She wondered who it could be, and then as they drew closer she knew.

"Lord, please give me patience," she muttered, recognizing the large black four-by-four truck in the lead. Clint Matlock had returned.

Tires screeching, he halted his truck in front of her building. The other vehicles followed suit. Clint and six men stepped to the pavement. Why, it looked like the shoot-out at the O.K. Corral. Scuffed boots, snug, work-worn jeans, sweat-soaked Stetsons… These were real cowboys! And they all stood, legs planted slightly apart, fist jammed on hard hips, staring up at her with steely eyes as if she were some kind of bandit. She felt like she should draw her six-shooter or something.

"I told you to get out of this heat." Clint's voice was dangerously low; his spurs clinked ominously as he stepped toward her.

Her pulse skipped about fifty beats—she plunked a hand to her hip and met his deadly glare. "And I told you I had to finish painting today." Goodness, but the man was gorgeous!

"Either you come down off that roof or I'm coming up and hauling you down."

The men looked from Clint to Lacy.

"Two things. One—I'd like to see you try hauling me down from here. And two—what are they doing here?

"*They* are going to finish this job for you. Now come on down. Or I'm warning you, I'm coming up."

The man was infuriating…and intriguing. He had to be the orneriest man she'd ever met in her entire life. Not many men had ever stood up to her for long. She admired Clint's courage. Plus, at least he'd brought help. She had begun to worry that all the cowpokes were worthless, like the ones that had watched her from across the street off and on all day. They hadn't even offered to help clean up the mess after Clint left. All they'd wanted to know was if Lacy and Sheri wanted to go for a beer when they finished work. The slugs. Automatically Lacy had relegated them to the bottom of her matchmaking list.

"Well, are you coming down or what?" Clint drawled, stepping toward the ladder.

"Don't you dare touch my ladder again. I'm coming down." Thrusting out her chin, she stalked to the ladder. There was no sense letting him know how much she appreciated his coming to her rescue. Or how much she needed rescuing.

Or how cute he was, doing the rescuing!

Watching Lacy descend the ladder, Clint figured he'd been a bit hasty coming back. The woman was dangerous to his mental health. She was trouble all right. He told himself not to get mixed up with her, but…every time he saw her, he liked what he saw. It wasn't only the looks that set her apart, it was her mouth. When she opened it and smarted off—well, he liked it. He kind of enjoyed the banter. But that didn't mean he wanted anything to come of it. Because he didn't.

She'd reached the bottom rung and was mere inches from him. Up close, she was flushed more than he'd first thought. Stubborn woman could be near a heat-stroke already.

"Cowboy," she said, cupping her palm against his jaw. He started at the surprise contact. "I can tell you're used to getting your way, people jumping at your every command. I've done it this time—" She dropped her hand and started walking up the steps to her salon. "But—" she paused at the door and looked over her shoulder at him "—I wouldn't get used to it if I were you."

The woman seriously impaired his thinking process. Clint shook his head and forced his gaze from the doorway through which Lacy had just disappeared. To think he'd rushed back to town to show some neighborly goodwill by helping paint her building. All the while telling himself he could handle being near her.

Her touch on his cheek had snagged his attention and set his skin to tingling, but it was the challenge in her words that had him wanting—what? Wanting to crowd her space and see what happened. That's what.

"Clint, you want us to start painting?"

"Yeah, that's what I want," he snapped, turning to his top hand, J.P. He'd walked over while Clint had been drowning in thoughts and now stood beside him staring up at the building in shock. "Get the boys started. I want this building painted by nightfall." Clint secured his hat firmly in place. It wouldn't do for the men to see his pink hair. He'd never get any work out of them for all the bad jokes and rank laughter. He tugged at his waistband and squared his shoulders before turning back toward the doorway. He and Lacy had some business to finish and he needed to make certain she hadn't walked into the cool building and passed out.

"Sir?"

He paused at the door and lifted an eyebrow at the bitter face the younger man was making. "Something bothering you, J.P.?"

"Well—" he shrugged a shoulder toward the building "—pink?"

Clint's sentiments exactly. "Yeah, pink," he said, then stomped into Lacy's flaming flamingo building.

He found her standing beside a small refrigerator downing a glass of water. Instantly his gut twisted at the sight of her, relaxed for the first time. After a moment he forced his gaze away to the safety of surveying the room.

What a mess! Wallpaper peeled away from one wall, another wasn't even drywalled! Instead, naked brick met his gaze. The floor was hardwood and very near ruination. Beat-up with age, it had been swept but would require more than the bristles of a broom to become presentable. The fifteen-foot ceiling wasn't much better with its ancient light fixtures off-kilter, some hanging by mere threads. At best, the place was a regular firetrap. If Lacy were half smart, she'd do herself a favor, toss a match to the place and walk away.

But obviously Lacy and her friend, who was squatted in a corner peeling paper, weren't half-smart. They were slap crazy.

"Don't you love it?"

Love it? He twisted, searching for what Lacy was speaking of, but she was looking at him and he knew, with startling regret, that the adoration in her voice wasn't aimed his direction. "You aren't talking about this place?"

She wiped the last of the perspiration from her forehead with a small white towel and smiled. "Well, what else would I be talking about? You?"

"Of course not," he said, jamming his hands in his pockets, confused as to why that statement bothered him so. He glanced around again at the mess and wondered at the kind of woman who could look past the dirt and grime and see something to love. "My men will finish painting the outside of the building. That way you can start work in here. Why? I don't know."

His sarcasm prompted a chuckle. "You think my place is a wreck?"

"A *wreck*—" he paused dramatically "—would be too kind a word." This statement garnered a dour look from her, and Clint found himself smiling. "You think I'm kidding?"

"Quite the contrary, I know you're dead serious."

He cocked a hip, mocking the way he'd seen her do many times. "Oh, yeah, how's that?"

She fanned herself with her hand. "If there's one thing I know, it's people. You took one look at this place and saw doom and gloom. Same as Sheri."

Clint figured on that point she had him, considering his lack of understanding of how anyone could look at such a dump in any other way.

He was in the process of saying so when her coloring went from flushed to pasty. She swayed, then started crumbling.

* * *

One minute Lacy was standing, then she was doubled over in a chair staring at old gum wads stuck to the underside of the seat while Clint Mad-dog Matlock held her head down and commanded her to breathe!

"Do what?" she cried, gasping for air—air that had been forced from her windpipe when he'd crushed her in his big-bear-rescue hug then slammed her into the gum-infested chair.

"Breathe, Lacy. The woozy feeling will pass after a minute."

"I told her to slow down."

That came from Sheri, who Lacy could see out of the corner of her upside-down view, had moved to the sink. From the sound she was wetting something down.

"You'll learn that Lacy does what Lacy wants." She continued. "It's a genetic screwup."

"I love you, too, Sheri," Lacy growled, struggling against Clint's powerful grip.

"Yeah, well, you need to," Sheri snapped, slapping a wet rag across the back of Lacy's neck. "Nobody but me would be fool enough to go along with your nonsense."

Lacy started a comeback, but rivers of water were running down her neck, up her jawbone and detouring straight into her nose—I'm drowning here!

"Haven't you ever heard of heatstroke?" Clint asked.

Heatstroke? I'm drowning! The man was completely oblivious to the fact that he was killing her. She managed to turn her head, to take a breath, and was about to do some talking of her own, when she noticed the warmth of Clint's strong fingers and the gentle pulsing movements they were making against her collarbone. She clamped her mouth firmly shut and shifted a tad into the feel of those hands. What nice hands he has….

"In this climate, you work a while and rest a while."

His voice had shifted to match the soothing rhythm of his hands.

"Especially if you aren't used to it," he continued.

He'd crouched to her level—mere inches from her—and suddenly, just like a moment in the movies she loved, Lacy felt suspended in time, drifting in the moment.

"I—" Clint started, cleared his throat and continued softly "—I work in the heat every day and I still have to call it quits when my body signals it's had enough."

He really had the most beautiful lips, strong lines sloped into a questioning frown. His hands, now still, remained on her collarbone, fanned out wide. Against everything she believed in and wanted, Lacy lifted her hand and touched the corner of his lips with the tip of her finger. And that's when she knew she could be in trouble here.

And that was simply not in her plans.

Chapter Six

Clint took a breath. He felt as if he were having heat-stroke himself looking at Lacy's lovely face. There was no denying that she was appealing.

His heart thudded when her gaze rested on his lips like a gentle butterfly, then flitted upward to meet his gaze.

Of its own accord, his hand lifted and pushed a damp swath of hair from her temple. "I," he started, shifting closer still. "I—"

"I'm sorry," she filled in, straightening suddenly. "I tend to be a bit headstrong. I didn't mean to cause you so much trouble." She was chattering. "And I called you all kinds of silly names—not to mention killing your Jeep. Can you forgive me?"

He swallowed a groan as she leaned in and pressed a kiss to his cheek.

What had he been thinking? He stumbled up and back like he'd been zapped with a cattle prod. "Stay put," he growled, backing toward the door, wanting to run before he did something really stupid like hauling her up and giving her a real kiss. "Don't venture out that door again today."

"But I have to finish. I need to be opened when the women start coming."

He paused at the door, savoring the look of her. "You really think this cockamamie scheme will work?"

"Not think—I *know* it's going to work."

Clint pushed his hat back a tad, feeling frustrated. "You don't say. Are you always so positive?"

A loud laugh rang out from Sheri, who had been silent until now. "If you only knew."

Lacy Brown was going to be the ruination of some poor fella. And it wouldn't be him, he reminded himself.

"Like I said," he said curtly, before Lacy could interrupt, "stay put. My men will take care of painting the outside. You work inside, out of the sun. It's safer that way."

Before she could say anything else—and he was certain she would—Clint spun on his heel and exited the building. He needed to cool off and get his head back on straight. He'd done his duty. He'd acted neighborly, had his men giving a helping hand and now he needed to get back to work. *His* work.

He didn't quite make it. Norma Sue halted him on the sidewalk. "Howdy-doody, Clint," she said, hurtling to a stop beside him. "Roy Don called and told me how neighborly you were being to Lacy. I think that's right nice of you. I thought the girls might like to come on over to the house for grilled burgers and fries later on tonight. Didn't think you'd mind, seeing how accommodating you've been."

Clint scowled. Norma Sue and Roy Don lived in the foreman's house on the ranch. It was just a hop, skip and a jump from his place. Lacy Brown on his territory—he wasn't all too lit up with the idea, but Norma Sue had a right to invite whoever she wanted. "Suit yourself. I'm tracking rustlers again tonight." He started to walk off.

"Now, Clint, hold on a minute. You know those coots will still be there after supper. You come on over and welcome these girls. Wouldn't be right if you didn't."

"Norma Sue—"

"Don't you Norma Sue me! I've changed your diapers and swatted your backside while you were waiting to fill your daddy's boots. He'd have come and so will you. It's the right thing to do."

The right thing to do for who? "I'll be there. But I'm not staying for coffee."

"Fine. I'm sure with a sweet thing like Lacy, I won't have any trouble getting one of your hired hands to come over for polite conversation after supper."

"Polite," Clint scoffed. "Have you met Lacy Brown? The woman wouldn't know polite if she fell in it." Well, that's not completely true.

Norma Sue chuckled. "This is good, Clint. Your feathers haven't been this riled up in…ever. Boy, you ain't had this happen to you before. Have you?"

"If by that you mean, have I ever met a woman made for trouble like that one in there? Then the answer would be no. Never. And I really don't reckon this time has made my day. I've been run over by a pink piece of junk. Had myself painted pink from head to toe by that little filly. Norma Sue—" he paused, shook his head "to be honest—I don't want to think about what comes next."

Trying to relax, Lacy drove toward Clint's ranch. However, she was tired and edgy. She seldom had a problem with energy, hyperactivity being a flaw she'd faced all her life. But tonight her sunburn stung and she felt physically drained. Not to mention that she was disappointed in herself. She had once again not shown a very Christian manner toward Clint Matlock.

"Sheri," she said loudly, talking over the wind whipping around them in the open convertible, "I hate to admit it, but I guess I stayed out in the sun too long."

"Uh-huh. You just now figured that out? Look at you. Our handsome neighbor probably really did save you from heatstroke."

Lacy frowned. She didn't like feeling foolish, but the worst was owing more thanks to Clint Matlock. The bullheaded ox—she could just see his smirk. There you go again.

The man was too domineering for his own good. Too sure of himself. Each time he came near, she felt like she'd just completed a twenty-mile race. *Dear Lord, I know part of the reason I'm reacting toward Clint this way is because I don't want to feel this attraction. So help me to ignore the physical feelings I'm having so that he might see You in me and not me in me.*

Her quick prayer done, she turned into the driveway of Norma Sue's place and shifted the Caddy into Park. Instantly she knew God had a funny sense of humor because Clint came striding up to the car the minute she turned off the ignition.

"How's the Caddy?" he asked, opening her door.

"Smart move," Sheri said, striding past him toward the porch. "Asking about that car is the way to her heart. That rattletrap has more dimples than my thighs, but Lacy loves it."

Lacy stepped from the car, reminding herself that she had a mission to complete and Clint was not a distraction she needed. "What? No name-calling?"

He shrugged, tipping his hat back a tad with his thumb in that now-familiar way of his. Those disturbing eyes settled on her.

"To each his own," he said dryly. "I figure you also have a picture of Elvis hanging in a prominent place on your wall."

"Doesn't everyone?" she teased, moving toward the porch, intent on getting away.

Clint's chuckle behind her was snuffed out by a burst of laughter from inside the house up ahead. Against her better judgment, Lacy slowed her pace on the pebbled path.

The short path snaked around a huge oak tree flanked by massive rosebushes. She paused beside the oak's twisted trunk. Clint paused beside her, and over the fragrant aroma of roses she caught the fresh, clean scent of soap. A clean soap smell had always been Lacy's favorite.

"So, why the infatuation for Elvis?"

Elvis? Who was Elvis? "It's not really," she said, trying to ignore Clint's nearness and the odd fact that he seemed to want to talk to her after he'd stormed out of her salon like she'd grown horns.

"I—I like his music," she stammered, glancing to the rose beside her, amazed at her trepidation. "He made wonderful music, but his life was a shambles." Looking up, she lifted an eyebrow at Clint. "I've always felt sorry for him. I tend to want to fix…things."

"So, you like to fix people?" He studied her intently.

Lacy lifted a shoulder and smiled. "It's a weakness I have."

"So you came to Mule Hollow to fix things? I hope you learned your lesson out there today. Any more stunts like that one this afternoon, and you'll be the one needing to be fixed."

So much for feeling all warm and fuzzy about the man. Lacy straightened her shoulders and met the infuriating man's gaze straight on. "I thank you very much for having your men finish painting for me this afternoon. However, I did fine before they got there, and I would have finished without them."

"You would have been in bed from that heatstroke I keep warning you about."

"Clint Matlock, you are the most irritating man I have ever met."

"Me? *Ha.*" He stepped closer and glared down at her from beneath the brim of his hat.

"Ha." Lacy snapped. Feeling like a prizefighter, she stepped up to Clint. "You are a high-handed domineering bully. If all the men in this town are half as bullheaded as you, then we can all forget this 'revive-the-town plan' right now. And as for you, you can forget about being included. I'm not even going to try and find you a mate. It would be impossible."

"And what makes you think I need *you* to help me find a woman?"

Lacy glanced to her right, then to her left, before locking eyes with him again. "I don't see any around here."

"Well, I'm busy," he grunted. "And I'm not interested in a ball and chain anyway."

"Yeah, right, get original," she added dryly. "That's what they all say."

"What about you? I don't see any men hanging on your arm, lady."

"So—" she paused, still glaring up at him "—I don't need a man hanging on my arm. I'm just fine on my own. I don't need that headache. I'm staying single for now."

"Well, little darlin'," he drawled as he turned away. His last words floated back to Lacy over his shoulder. "That shouldn't be too hard."

Ohhh…she wanted to throw something. She held in a scream and watched him saunter up the steps and into the house. How dare he imply that she couldn't find a husband if she wanted to. She could. She really could. If she wanted. *Couldn't I, Lord?*

"Lacy Brown," Norma Sue yelled, from behind the screen door, "come on in here, girl."

She took a deep breath and sniffed. Of course she wasn't crying. She never did such a thing. It was tension. Or allergies. "I'm coming, Norma Sue. You sure have some nice roses." She hurried to the porch, up the wooden steps and through the open door. *Dear Lord, please tell me what's going on here.*

"Clint," Norma Sue boomed across the room a few moments later. He leaned against the mantel talking with Sheri and a cowboy who had helped paint the salon earlier. "What were you thinking, leaving Lacy out on the porch all alone? What happened to your manners?"

"Lacy's an independent woman. She didn't want me holding the door open for her."

"Clint—"

"Norma Sue, Clint is right," Lacy broke in. "I'm a big girl. I can take care of myself."

Norma Sue looked skeptically from one to the other. Then her face split open with a wide grin. "I imagine you can. Come on in here and meet Roy Don and J.P. Then we'll head out back to eat on the deck."

Lacy wasn't too sure she liked Norma's smile. Like she knew something Lacy didn't. Well, if she thought the sparks flying tonight were of a romantic nature, then she was wrong. Dead wrong. Clint Matlock could eat his hat.

What kind of fool was she? Lacy asked herself a few hours later. She was stranded on the side of the road with an empty tank of gas and a long, dark way to walk.

Clint had left Norma Sue's shortly after finishing his meal, and then J.P. had given Sheri a ride home. Esther and Adela had arrived before dinner so Lacy stayed and talked about plans for Mule Hollow. Lacy had disclosed her desire to paint all the buildings along Main Street bright colors. She'd been happy when they understood her motivation and had offered to petition the townfolk for the money to buy all the paint. They also assured her that there would be plenty of cowboys who would show up to help with the painting. They had volleyed ideas back and forth until the wee hours of the morning, so excited that they could actually visualize the renewing of Mule Hollow. They also agreed that the ad campaign would need to continue and Adela volunteered to come up with booth ideas at the fair to raise money for the fund.

When they'd all finally headed home, Lacy was keyed up. Far too restless for sleep, she'd taken a drive in the country.

Driving or jogging always relaxed her. As an overactive child, she'd had trouble sleeping. Her mother learned early that a ride in the car lulled her to sleep. Though money had always been scarce, her mother had always managed to keep enough gas in the tank so Lacy could get the rest she needed. Now, driving simply relaxed her and gave her joy. She liked driving with the top down. Feeling the cool breeze on her skin and in her hair prepared her for bed like a gentle massage. She also found that that was when the Lord spoke to her.

He hadn't spoken tonight. He seemed to have abandoned her instead, since she was stranded in the middle of nowhere, flat out of gas. Gas she was sure was there before supper. And the Lord was nowhere in sight.

Nothing was. The moon's earlier light was now hidden behind a heavy overcast sky. Shadows loomed everywhere.

A strange mournful howl filled the night air. A shiver raced down Lacy's spine. "I'm not scared. I'm not scared," she chanted, rubbing her arms. "Just a coyote looking for love," she mumbled.

Midnight drives down well-lit city streets, she was used to, not dark country roads. Searching uneasily through the darkness, she could barely see the white stripe on the pavement. She prided herself on not being easily frightened; however, it wouldn't hurt if the shadows lifted a bit. Better yet, she wished clicking her heels together three times would get her home and into her warm bed. The chances of that happening or of a car showing up were about even.

She had never felt farther away from the Lord than in that instant. That was a feeling she could not take.

She began to pray. *Oh, Lord, Father, You have my attention. Please forgive me for my many transgressions, especially the ones involving Clint Matlock. I'll try to watch my temper around him and show You through me. I'm sorry I'm having such a hard time doing that. It seems I keep promising You one thing and then turning around and blowing it. I'll do better, but obviously I can't do it on my own. Please help. Now,*

about me here in the dark, I'm kind of scared and won-
der if You could please get me home safely. In Your
name and will to be done I pray, amen.

Stiffening her spine and feeling better, she started
walking. She hadn't taken two steps when a loud clap
of thunder split the sky open and rain poured down
upon her.

"Oh, not now," she sputtered, looking heavenward.
She knew Texas weather was unpredictable, but this
was ridiculous! She was drenched in a matter of seconds as she hurried back to the Caddy and tried rais-
ing the roof. It was stuck, and helplessly she watched
as the floorboard started filling with water.

"Great. Just *great,*" she yelled. Another blast of
thunder rebuked her, roaring through the night. "Okay,
Lord," she squeaked. "What are You trying to teach
me?" Looking around for some kind of shelter, she
found nothing. She couldn't have seen anything anyway if it had been right under her nose, it was so dark.

Okay, Lord, now what? She lifted her face to the
rain. The plump drops plopped and pounded her skin,
rolling over her like cool water from a sprinkler. A
mind-jolting crack of thunder rocked Lacy from her
thoughts and propelled her to action and she started
walking.

Her white sundress slapped about her calves, her
sandals flopped against the soles of her feet and her
hair turned into a sopping mop that kept sliding over

her eyes. She had walked about a mile when a cool breeze blew in and she started shivering uncontrollably.

After the second mile she reached a bridge that only hours before had been over a small gurgling stream. Now, it was covered by a raging flood.

Lord, Lord, why are You doing this to me? she questioned, utterly deflated. Her optimism plummeted. What was she going to do? She could try to cross in her sandals, but the water was flowing so rapidly, she couldn't be certain of her footing. If she'd worn her jeans and boots she would have at least had adequate protection against things that might cut her feet beneath the water. But nooo! Not tonight. She had chosen to wear a dress. It really made her mad when she had realized earlier in her stroll that she'd chosen the dress to impress Clint Matlock.

Tales of people drowning while attempting to cross floodwaters passed through her mind, but she knew she had to do something.

"Think positive, Lacy. Think. Someone will come looking for me. Sheri will send someone to find me." Except their phone hadn't been connected yet. She took a shuddering breath, fighting back the tears in her waterlogged eyes. Thunder clapped again, causing her to jump before turning and heading back toward her car.

Gloomy images of being found the following morning, bloated and blue, floated before her. She sniffled and swiped at her nose. She'd had such high hopes when she'd come to Mule Hollow. Now look where she was, on a deserted road on foot. Alone. And other than Sheri, not one person would miss her if she didn't make it home.

Chapter Seven

Clint halted his truck at the far edge of the bridge that stood between him and the road leading home. He'd kept his word and left Norma Sue's early, going to the back pasture in the hope of catching the rustlers in the act of stealing his cattle. The fact that he'd also been escaping from Lacy Brown didn't count. But images had followed him. Images of her in that white dress. Of the way it flowed about her like a gentle caress. Of the way her eyes sparkled in challenge when he'd goaded her. Even before the rain began to fall, he'd lost interest in rustlers.

Now, as usual after a disappointing night, he wanted a fresh cup of coffee and a warm bed. And dreamless sleep. Through his racing windshield wipers he gauged the depth of the rising water, shifted his truck into gear and eased the big four-wheel-drive forward. His vehicle was made to handle rough country, to pass through hazards when most cars and trucks had to turn away. Still, he proceeded with caution. Even though he knew this bridge, knew it was built to withstand these seasonal floods, he understood he was taking a risk. Once on the other side, anxious to get home, he pressed the accelerator. He'd gone about two miles when suddenly out of nowhere a misty shape appeared in the center of the road. He yanked hard on the steering wheel, only to be met by the looming pink form of Lacy Brown's ridiculous Cadillac. Slamming on his brakes, he gave one last powerful pull on the wheel and prayed he didn't hit anything or anybody.

Out of control, the mammoth truck skidded and twisted until it came to a jerking halt deep in a muddy ditch. Unharmed, Clint sprang from the cab and hit the mud running, hoping and still praying that he'd missed the person he'd seen staggering down the center of the lane. It must have been Lacy Brown.

Lightning sizzled across the sky, immediately followed by a thunderous boom that rocked the ground. In the flash of light, he caught sight of the apparition frozen at the side of the road.

"Lacy?" he yelled in disbelief over the howling wind. "Lacy Brown?" What was she doing out in the middle of nowhere?

"C-Clint—"

The strangled sob reached him just as another clap

of thunder and bolt of lightning ripped across the night. She flung herself across the ten yards separating them and into his arms. She was freezing and shivering uncontrollably. How long had she been trapped in this flash flood? He didn't stop to ask her questions, but lifted her easily in his arms and hurried back to his truck. He knew he had to get her out of the storm.

"I th-thought I'd killed you," she whispered through chattering teeth.

"Shh," he murmured against her ear, hugging her harder to his chest. "You're safe now."

"S-stupid of m-me," she stuttered, still shivering.

"No, not stupid. The weather out here is unpredictable. There was a chance of rain in the forecast. Not a flash flood."

He made it to the truck without slipping in the mud and managed to get them both into the cab without falling. He'd left the engine running, so he immediately tried to back out of the deep ditch, but his four-wheel drive wasn't engaging. Something seemed to have snapped in the crash.

"I'm not good luck for y-you."

Her voice was a hoarse whisper. A chord inside Clint's chest tightened. Reaching out, he pulled her cold body against him. "We have to get you out of those wet clothes so you'll warm up." He rummaged behind the seat of the truck and pulled out a crumpled denim work shirt. "This thing is a mess but it's pretty clean. It was too hot to work in yesterday, so I worked in my T-shirt instead. You can put it on and then use my sleeping bag to wrap up in. You'll warm up in no time."

A slight nod and a shiver were all she managed as she accepted the shirt. Clint turned on the heater to help get the chill out of the air then reached past her for the sleeping bag he'd brought for the long night he'd expected to spend waiting and watching for rustlers. His thermos of coffee lay next to the bag.

"I'll get out of the truck and give you some privacy while you change out of that dress. Here, I'll unroll the sleeping bag for you, use it for more privacy if you want to. Can you manage all right?" She was shaking so bad it worried him as he shook out the sleeping bag.

As if refuting his concern, she nodded, "I can do it. You're going to get wet, though." Her eyes were as big as the moon.

"I'll be fine." He reached under the seat and pulled out his slicker. "Honk the horn when you're done. I'll come back and we can have some hot coffee." Wrenching his gaze away from her pale face, he pushed open the door and stepped into the rain. He yanked on the slicker and stomped through the mud to stand beside the road, contemplating their situation while the rain washed over him.

It took her about ten minutes to change. When she

honked the horn, he was more than ready to climb back into the warm, dry truck.

"I can't believe how cold I am. In the dead of s-summer," she chattered.

Clint could see her arms as she spread her dress on the dash of his truck. "It's your sunburn plus the wind chilling the rain," he said, glad he'd found her before she'd been exposed to the night any longer. He'd only been out in the downpour briefly, but he was feeling the chill, too.

She had his thick shirt buttoned to the neck and he could tell at a glance that it totally swallowed her.

Despite having burrowed into the depths of the sleeping bag, she was still shivering and pale. Exhaustion etched on her usually animated face. The night's ordeal had taken its toll on her, and Clint wanted nothing more in that moment than to see all the energy he'd grown used to seeing bubble out of Lacy return.

At odds with himself, he poured her a cup of coffee. "Drink this," he said gruffly. Her fingers shook, taking the cup from him. Automatically he wrapped his hands around hers and lifted the cup to her lips.

When her lips brushed his fingers as she took a sip of the steaming brew, he froze. There was no way he could deny the chemistry between them. Lacy's gaze met his and he knew without doubt she felt the same.

He didn't want this.

"Thanks," she said quietly, looking away to the rain pounding against the window. "I'm not sure what I would have done if you hadn't—" her voice wobbled "—hadn't shown up."

Dear Lord—his quick prayer was stopped by the disarming, vulnerability in her eyes. She looked away, and he sensed she didn't like feeling weak. Couldn't tolerate it.

And that made him want to reach and brush a damp curl from her forehead. He didn't, though, suspecting she wouldn't appreciate that, either. Instead he said, "You would have thought of something." It was true. He'd only known her for a few days, but he knew nothing would hold Lacy Brown down for long. Though she'd had a few mishaps since coming to Mule Hollow, he had no doubt that she could take care of herself. It was obvious she was a strong woman in a small package. Wacky, but strong.

He poured her another cup of coffee and handed it to her. Her hand trembled again as she accepted the cup, but she offered him a weak smile of thanks before taking a sip and looking back into the night. The sound of the storm raging about them, the constant barrage on the windows cocooned them, as if they were standing behind a turbulent waterfall, cut off from the world.

"It seems like you're always saving me," she said softly, nervously.

Clint chuckled uneasily. "All in a day's work, ma'am."

Lacy shifted in the blanket. "So what now?" she asked, taking a long, slow breath.

Clint studied the night. It was safer than looking at Lacy. "We wait for the rain to let up then I'll go for help."

"I'll go with you," she practically sang.

That sounded more like the Lacy he knew. But she wasn't coming. "No way. It's too dangerous, and it'll be a miracle if you don't catch pneumonia as it is." He met her wide gaze and hung on to his guns with everything he had.

Looking into Clint's eyes, Lacy was suddenly aware of the solitude of their situation, of the rain pounding out its rhythmic music on the roof. The stubborn man. His eyes crinkled around the edges as he turned away. She watched him pull his hat low over his eyes, hunch his shoulders over the steering wheel and stare into the night.

Something inside her knotted up. For a moment the intensity of the feeling threatened to start a flow of tears. Confused by the strength of her reaction to Clint, she watched the muscle of his jaw tighten and relax. A tense silence settled around them. She wished for the rain to stop, so they could escape the confines of the truck and she could clear her mind and concentrate on her mission.

After a while Clint cleared his throat. "So, why did you choose Mule Hollow?"

His question was soft; it surprised her. It also gave her a focus other than the man sitting beside her. She latched on to the subject change with everything she had.

"Have you ever wanted something with all your heart?"

Clint didn't answer, just looked at her funny and then nodded. One quick defined nod and then he looked away again.

Lacy swallowed. "Me, too. Only, the whole picture wouldn't snap into place. Like, I knew I wanted to open my own salon. I saved every cent I could for four years, waiting on the right opportunity. There were times when I thought I'd found the right place. But things never worked out and the plans would fall apart."

Clint turned to watch her and Lacy smiled, feeling self-conscious about telling him such personal things. Things only Sheri knew. "And then last year I gave all the baggage of my life over to the Lord, and He set me free from all of it, my past hurts and sins. I began looking for a ministry immediately, and that's when the big picture started to come into focus. It had been there for me all along and I hadn't seen it or been ready for it." Excited at the recollection, she turned toward Clint, beaming. "I had a ministry right in my own backyard as the saying goes, right there under my nose. I could have a wonderful ministry standing behind the chair cutting hair."

"You see, I admire Paul in the Bible so much. His zeal at ministering to people, his obedience is humbling to me. He gave up so much and was so single-minded in his purpose. I wanted that, too, so I started praying fervently for direction…and then I ran across Adela's ad…" She paused, remembering the feeling that had overcome her reading the ad for the first time. "And God spoke to me. And I knew—I knew that Mule Hollow was where He would have me come."

Clint gave her a lopsided smile, and in the shadows of his hat brim thrown by the pale light from the dash, his eyes glinted. Lacy's stomach did a flip-flop.

"Of course Sheri thought I was crazy." She laughed nervously. "But what else is new? You see, I don't know if you noticed, but I'm a bit like Peter instead of Paul. I'm kind of headstrong and I put my foot in my mouth a lot."

Clint chuckled. "No, I hadn't noticed that at all."

"Look, bucko," she said, grinning and feeling weirdly at ease, "laugh all you want, but Mule Hollow will be everything I see in here." She tapped her forehead. "If you could only see what I see when I look down Main Street."

"I'm afraid to see what you see.'

"You just wait," she huffed.

"I already have, thanks to you." He tugged at his hat, securing it to his head. "Believe me, pink is not my color."

Lacy smiled, remembering him doused in pink paint. "No. I guess it isn't."

A comfortable silence stretched between them, and feeling relaxed, Lacy snuggled against the seat. The sound of the rain beating on the window beside her head was hypnotic. She hadn't slept well for days; now the rain, the heat exhaustion she'd felt earlier and her ordeal before Clint rescued her, all overwhelmed her. Of their own will, her eyes closed.

"And a husband? That isn't part of your dream? Your vision?"

His voice echoed as if through a long tunnel. "I don't need a husband," she answered without opening her eyes. "My dad ruined my mom's dreams." She yawned, snuggled deeper into the sleeping bag. "No man is getting the chance to take my dreams—" She yawned. "I want to be single-minded in my quest for God…like Paul." She managed to lift her eyelids briefly and met Clint's brooding, dark stare. Then her lashes drifted down and sleep captured her.

In the darkness, Clint listened to the soft slow rhythm of Lacy's breathing. Sleep had overcome her quickly; her words had slurred and then she was out. It seemed she was an all-or-nothing-type person. She ran on high-octane fuel, and when the tank ran out, the tank ran out. He found the idea touching. He knew that when she woke she'd be her raring-to-go, drive-a-man-crazy-self again…she did drive him crazy.

The thought wasn't at all what he wanted to think.

He knew that the less time he spent in the cab of his truck with her, the better off he'd be. Listening to the gentle sounds of her slumber was not easy on his mind. He wanted the rain to stop. He wanted out of his truck, and no matter how many times his mind wondered about how it would feel to kiss Lacy Brown, he wanted to get her home and away from him.

She was everything he didn't want in a woman. Everything…well, maybe not everything. He liked her sense of humor, her love of life, her love of the Lord…. Not many women out there wanted to be like Paul. He smiled. She was like Peter though. In his mind's eye he saw Peter stepping out into that turbulent water, not thinking about anything except getting to Jesus. Clint saw Lacy hopping over the side of the boat in the same manner she hopped over the door of her precious Caddy, intent only on getting to her Savior. The picture brought another smile to his lips.

Here he was, stuck in a ditch in the dead of night, and he was smiling. Since Lacy had blasted into town, he'd smiled more than he'd smiled in years.

He glanced into the darkness and studied the night. Did he want to smile? He rubbed the back of his neck, glancing in Lacy's direction. Thoughts of his mother intruded suddenly. What if Lacy was just a flighty gal, who everyone thought was something she really wasn't? What if everything she'd said was a lie?

Clint knew he needed out of the truck. If she was

the real thing, he needed to protect her from small-town talk. On the other hand, if she was every man's nightmare, he needed to be away from her, because by no choice of his own, he'd been through one nightmare with his mother and all of her lies.

He wasn't ready to volunteer for a second round of heartbreak.

Something woke Lacy. A soft murmur, her own sigh, something. She eased up in the seat, pulling the sleeping bag securely about her. Clint sat rigidly, staring out across the night. Beneath the hat, his expression was stone hard. She followed the direction of his attention to where a faint light bobbed on the midnight horizon.

"What is that?" she asked, rubbing her eyes with her fist. She was embarrassed that she'd fallen asleep instead of waiting out the storm with her eyes open. The least she could do was keep Clint company; it was after all her fault that he was in this situation.

"Rustlers, is what that is."

"What?"

"Cattle thieves. I'd decided they weren't going to move tonight. I guess I was wrong."

"Are they taking your cows?"

"Right now, as we speak."

"And you're just sitting here? Come on, let's go get them."

Clint turned to stare at her in disbelief. "We're stuck and a sleeping bag and a shirt, no matter how huge, is not rustler-hunting attire."

She'd forgotten that her dress was draped over the dash. "I'll put my dress back on," she said, reaching out and touching the fabric. "It's pretty dry. I'll put it on and we can sneak over there and see where they're going."

"Lacy, that's probably fifteen acres between us, and at least three fences."

"Don't you want to stop these guys?"

"Well, sure—"

"Then look out the window. We're outta here."

Clint shot her a quick glance. Lacy laughed. "Anybody ever tell you that you have absolutely no sense of humor, Clint Matlock?"

"This isn't funny."

"Yes, it is. You just can't see it. Now hold this sleeping bag up."

Obviously not happy Clint took the sleeping bag anyway and held it up. She made quick work of pulling on the damp dress; for added warmth she put his shirt back on over the dress. "Okay. Let's go."

"Lacy, we aren't going after them tonight."

"Why not? The rain stopped. The moon is coming out."

"We aren't going. We're on the backside of my homestead. We'll walk through the back roads. There's a small bridge we can cross and then we can get to my house. I'll take you home from there."

"I don't want to go home." How could he think about going home? She opened the door against his objections and stepped barefoot into the mud, ignoring the icky feel as it pressed into her toes. Since she was already a mess, with her hair plastered to her skull, her dress a dingy bit of ruined cloth, she paid the mud little mind. After all, muddy feet didn't mean much—she was going to catch rustlers! How cool was that? "Come on, Clint. I want to catch some cow rustlers."

"*Cattle* rustlers," he corrected dryly. "Here," he said a few seconds later, coming up to stand beside her at the fence. He shoved a pair of rubber boots at her, followed by a rag and a pair of socks. "These rubber boots are going to swallow your tiny feet, but they're dry and maybe you can manage to walk in them."

"Where'd all of this come from?"

He lifted one powerful shoulder, "I work in pastures—my feet get messed up a lot. It's always smart to keep a dry pair of socks and rubber boots on hand. If you hadn't been in such a hurry, I would have given them to you before."

"Sorry, but thank you. Thank you very much." Holding on to his arm for support, she wiped off most of the mud with the rag, then after some assistance from Clint, she pulled on the socks, then the boots. Clint didn't say anything, simply stood beside her, assisting in keeping her from falling flat on her face in the mud. Finally she straightened and took a few steps. The boots *were* huge, and at first Lacy feared she wouldn't be able to manage walking in them. But after a few awkward steps, adjusting to the slippy heel-toe/heel-toe clomping, she got the rhythm and did fairly well. Although, the boots weren't only large in foot size, they were also tall, brushing the bottom of her dress with each clumsy step she took. She knew she looked scary, but at least now she could walk, make that *stumble,* through the wet pasture, without mud oozing between her toes.

"Coming," she said, glancing back over her shoulder.

Clint scowled. "All right, but only because I want to catch those bozos so bad. They'll probably be gone before we get there."

He started ahead of her then whirled around. "One thing! You will do as I say, when I say, Lacy Brown or no go."

Lacy slammed her hands on her hips and glared at him. "What's the deal here? Does everyone have to take orders from you?"

"Not everybody. But if this little deal is going down then you'd better listen up. Or I'll have to hog-tie you."

She narrowed her eyes. "I'd like to see you try."

Clint stepped closer. In the moonlight she could see his sharp gaze. "Honey," he drawled, "you don't want to tangle with me."

"Oh, yeah, Clint Matlock," she snapped over the roar of her blood in her ears. "Is that a challenge?"

"No. *This* is a challenge," he said. He startled her by placing his hands on her shoulders, then he kissed her.

Kissed her! Lacy's heart thundered, suddenly she wasn't brave. She wanted to step away, frightened by the emotions raging through her. What had she done, challenging him?

As quickly as the kiss started, it ended. Clint dropped his hands, stepped away from her then strode toward the road. Baffled by what had happened between them, Lacy followed him, as best she could in the Texas-size rubber boots. When she reached him, he was staring at the pavement with his back to her. She studied the tense cords of his back, and shame overcame her. She had practically goaded him into that kiss. How could she have acted that way?

"I'm really sorry, Clint. I acted like a child. Will you forgive me?"

He swung around, and in the moonlight she saw surprise in his eyes. "You don't have anything to be sorry for. I'm the buffoon who grabbed you. There is no excuse for my behavior. None."

His unexpected remorse touched her. "Boy, do you know how to deflate a girl's ego. I'd like to think that I'm irresistible."

He chuckled and her stomach flipped. "Okay, so my

irresistibility didn't drive you to kiss me. So let's say it was due to a very stressful night that's never going to end if we don't get going and stop all this jabbering. We have rustlers to catch, remember."

Clint reached for her arm. "Lacy, look. I want to catch the rustlers, but this isn't the night to do it. Wait." He placed two fingers across her lips, silencing her protest. "We have enough ahead of us tonight without chasing down criminals who may not even be out there by the time we make it across the pastures."

Lacy's traitorous heart was skipping around in her chest at the feel of his touch. But it was her mind that surprised her, because she actually agreed with him. Not that she didn't want to hunt rustlers—she did— but she'd put Clint through enough for one day and night. It *was* time to go home. Or at least, time to try to get home before daybreak.

"You're right, Clint Matlock. Lead the way."

The surprise on his face at her compliance was comical, and she couldn't help teasing him. "Okay, you stand there with your mouth open, and I'll lead the way." She clomped away from him, dirty dress swishing.

In one stride, he fell into step beside her. "Lacy Brown, you are the most unpredictable woman I have ever met."

It surprised Lacy that she would have preferred irresistible to unpredictable.

Chapter Eight

"Do what?"

Lacy stared at the black swirling water that hid a bridge somewhere beneath its surface. Clint didn't blame her skepticism. The waters were treacherous. "I want you to hang on to my waist, my belt actually, and follow me across the bridge."

In the dim light of the moon, that kept appearing intermittently, Clint saw fear flicker across her face before she hid it with serious scrutiny. She'd followed him for the past half hour in silence—amazingly! Now her silence bothered him. "Lacy, it'll be all right. I won't let anything happen to you."

She raised her eyes and Clint thought it would kill him not to kiss her again. She *was* nearly irresistible.

"I know that," she said. "I'm just a bit nervous."

"I'm nervous, too," he admitted. "But if we don't

cross, we'll have to spend the night in my truck. And you know that's not right."

She contemplated the idea, studying the water, while nibbling on her lower lip.

Finally, with that quick all-or-nothing manner he'd come to admire in her, she nodded toward the water. "Lead the way. I never was much of a camper."

That's my Lacy, he thought. "I'll bet if you wanted to, you could be." When had she become his Lacy?

She smiled. "Do you want to spend the night in your truck?"

He was a Christian, and he knew the temptation and confusion being that close to her caused him. "It might be dangerous. People might talk."

Her smile broadened. "Cowboy, that's exactly why I wanted to cross the bridge. The Lord and I have big plans for Mule Hollow and tangoing with you is not part of them."

"And what Lacy Brown wants—" he murmured, suddenly wanting to hit something, "Lacy Brown gets."

"That's right." Her lip trembled. "At least most of the time, if it's the Lord's will."

Clint tucked a stray wisp of hair behind her ear.

"Now hold on tight, and whatever you do, don't let go. The danger isn't the depth but the swiftness of the floodwater. If it knocks you down, it could sweep you off the bridge—there isn't a railing."

"Believe me, I'll hang on, but I think we need to say a prayer."

"Sure," he agreed. He watched her bow her head and he did the same as she began her prayer.

"Dear Abba, forgive me where I've failed You today and help me to be a better steward in the hours to come. What a night You've given us. It's been tiring, but exciting, and You know how I like excitement. Thank You for sending Clint to help me, and for bringing us this far safely. I pray that we make it to the other side of this bridge in one piece so that tomorrow we can talk about what a great adventure we had tonight. Thank You for watching over us. I ask these things only if Your will be done. Amen."

"That was an interesting prayer. You talked to God like he was your dad or your friend."

"He is on both counts," she said gently.

Clint prayed, but not like Lacy. His dad had always said more formal prayers, and as a kid growing up he'd learned by that example. Turning toward the rushing waters he quickly said his own prayer and tried Lacy's approach for himself. Peace settled around him, as if he were speaking to friend. A friend above all others.

"Okay, let's do this," Lacy said from behind him. She grasped his leather belt tightly and he heard her inhale deeply.

"Here we go. Hang on." *This is it, Lord. Keep her*

safe, please, he thought, then stepped into the water, wishing there were a railing. Lacy followed and he waited, letting her adjust to the feel of the water surging against her legs. Her grasp tightened on his belt and he stepped farther out into the rushing water, adjusting to the strength of the current. One minute Lacy was there and the next she gasped and let go of his belt. Clint spun and in a horrified effort, grabbed for her.

But she was gone, swept out of reach by the swirling currents.

Like a guppy swimming upstream, Lacy flopped and foundered in the surprisingly strong water, already a foot deep on the bridge. The raging current swept her mercilessly toward the bridge's edge as she tried, clawing and choking, to find something to grab onto.

Suddenly a strong hand wrapped around her wrist and held fast. The next instant she was pulled from the water and into Clint's secure arms. He held her tightly while her heart hammered, and she gagged and sputtered and probably bawled. Her life had just flashed before her eyes with pitiful accuracy, and suddenly all she wanted was to be held by Clint Matlock.

"If you think I'm giving you another chance to save me, you're wrong," she muttered against his neck, absorbing the wondrous feel of his heart, pounding near to hers. Standing in the center of the bridge, his feet planted firmly on the wood, like a solid pillar withstanding the raging waters, he held her securely. It hit her that this was a picture of how life with Clint Matlock would always be.

Wordlessly he began moving toward the bank. His strength evident in his movements through the current. Lacy couldn't have put her feet back in that water if she'd wanted to, but she didn't get the chance. He held her snugly against him and managed the crossing within minutes. When at last they walked onto dry ground, she wanted to kiss him. Who was she kidding! She wanted to marry him and have his children! *Dear Father, what have You done to me?*

"Since I've come to Mule Hollow, I'm not certain who's in the most danger. You or me," she croaked.

He placed his forehead against hers. "I knew the moment I first saw you that you were trouble. I've been saying it at least twice a day ever since." His voice was gruff, his hand gentle as he smoothed her hair. Shifting away from her, he studied her face, then lowered her to the ground. "Can you manage?" he asked, still holding her tight against him.

Her feet barely touched the pavement, and Lacy felt like laughing. She'd read love stories, knew about significant moments when the hero and heroine shared their feelings through eye contact. And she knew she wasn't supposed to laugh.

But *this isn't a love story.* "You're asking me if I can

manage? Me. Klutzola. To be honest, I'm not sure what I can do anymore. Maybe barefooted, I can manage to walk the rest of the way without falling."

"And maybe you can't," he said, and swept her back into his arms and started walking. "I should never have risked you walking across that bridge."

"Clint, put me down," she sputtered. "I can walk." He didn't stop.

She didn't want him to carry her. She wanted to walk on her own feet. If she weren't careful, she'd forget all about her mission and fall flat out in love with the guy.

Talk, the talk Clint had so sweetly wanted to protect her from, spread like ice melting near an open flame. By the time Lacy woke the next morning, Norma Sue, Esther Mae and Adela were waiting on her doorstep.

The first thing Lacy saw when she answered the door was Esther Mae's triple-decker doing a shimmy as she shook her head vigorously to something Norma Sue had just said. All three of them clammed up, staring innocently at Lacy the minute she opened the door. Something was up.

"Come in and give me the scoop. What's on the grapevine this morning?" Standing aside, she let the ladies scurry into the living room.

"What scoop?" Norma Sue asked innocently.

Lacy perched on the edge of her flowered couch. Her neon yellow nightshirt blended well with the fluorescent kaleidoscope of colors in the couch's print. "Now, Norma Sue, I know you don't know me very well. Yet, I would hope you realize that I give my opinion and thoughts straight out. I expect the same in return. Now, what's on your minds?"

"Is what Norma Sue says true?" Adela asked.

"Yeah. Did you spend the night with Clint?"

The question startled Lacy, even though she'd half expected it. Their expressions told exactly what they were thinking. Shame on them.

"Oh, come on, girls," Lacy said. "Of course not. My car ran out of gas then the storm blew in and drenched me. Clint *kind of* rescued me."

"Kind of?" Esther Mae asked. Crestfallen, she looked at Adela then Norma Sue. Even her hair seemed to droop. "How do you *kind of* rescue someone?"

Lacy related her story—omitting the kissing. She wasn't *not* giving the story to them straight, she simply didn't believe certain parts of the evening were everybody's business. Since there were parts of last night that she didn't understand herself, she had no great desire to pass the confusing and private details down the grapevine.

"Well, what happened after y'all made it to his house?" Norma Sue asked.

"He brought me home, then he went home." Again,

Lacy didn't think the ladies needed to know how strained the ride home had been.

And they certainly didn't need to know just how disappointed she'd been when he'd turned away and driven off without following through with another kiss.

Just a few short hours after dropping Lacy off at her house, Clint was sitting at his desk whistling as he thumbed through a week's worth of unopened mail. Between rustlers and Lacy Brown, opening mail had been the last thing on his mind. But it had to be done, and after last night's unbelievable events, sitting down at his desk for mail call held even less appeal.

Lacy Brown intrigued him. No matter how much he wanted to deny it, he couldn't. Maybe, just maybe, she wasn't just a flighty, looking-for-fun gal. She really did seem to have real substance. No matter what he told himself, she seemed to be the total package.

Seemed being the pivotal word.

He tapped the corner of the envelope on his desktop and wrangled with the desire to forget the pain in his past. Right now all he wanted to do was haul his carcass into town and hold Lacy again.

Even if it went against every good brain cell he had in his head.

Absentmindedly, he glanced down at the letter in his hand. He'd been sorting the many envelopes into piles, as he had to get some work done. Skimming over the return address, he was ready to deposit it into its appropriate stack of bills, personal or ranch correspondence, when the name on the upper left-hand corner jumped out at him. Clint's world tilted as he forced himself to focus on the name in neat script: Amber Matlock. His mother's name stared back at him. She'd used her name as it had been all those years ago, when she'd still been his mother, when she'd still had the right to carry his father's last name. White-hot anger flashed through Clint; she had no right to the Matlock name now, not after the shame she'd brought to it. He dropped the letter, scraped his chair back and away, glaring at the plain white envelope. His heart pounded, and there was a surge in his blood pressure that the three feet between him and the letter did nothing to ease.

How many times as a kid had he wished to see his mother's name on an envelope addressed to him? How many times had he prayed she'd come home?

Rocked to his core, he reached out, picked up the envelope and slowly turned it over in his palm. He was a grown man, and yet he felt transported back in time to that same hurting kid he'd been when his mother had chosen someone else over him. No goodbye, no word…ever. Until now. His gut ached; emotions he'd fought hard to suppress slammed into him in hard waves.

After years of wondering, years of wishing… His

hand trembled with weakness as another wave hit him. What did she want? Was she all right? Fighting back the betraying curiosity, the longing he'd thought he'd overcome, he slowly, very slowly pulled open his desk drawer, dropped the letter inside and slammed it shut with a definite thud.

The silence that echoed through the room held un-asked questions. Questions he did not care to give voice to. His mother had torn his childish heart to shreds when she'd left him.

Because of that he'd stopped wishing for anything that had to do with Amber Matlock a long time ago.

And that was how it would remain.

Chapter Nine

Lacy had been working hard in the salon for three days since Clint rescued her from the flash flood. Thanks to his ranch hands, the painting had been done in record time and the windows had been washed and shined. J.P. had helped Sheri hang the light fixtures straight, then Lacy had whitewashed the beat up wood floor. The ragged building now looked like a new place. It had a welcoming ambiance that pleased Lacy. All it needed was a bit of wallpaper, a couple of shampoo bowls hooked up and a mirror hung, and they would be ready for business.

Though he had sent his cowhands to help, Clint hadn't come back into town since that stormy night. It had probably been for the best, because she hadn't been able to get him off her mind. There were quite a few things about that night that she couldn't forget. The kiss, the way he'd held her, the way she'd felt when he'd held her. But the way she'd felt when he'd reached into that surging water and pulled her from danger was the kicker. Everything in her perspective had shifted after that experience. She'd already had trouble getting the picture of him standing in the center of the road the day of their first meeting out of her head, his chin tucked to his chest, his head cocked so that his dark gaze angled upward at her as he asked if she was looking for a husband. Now, that question replayed in her mind like a chant.

She had been in Mule Hollow just shy of two weeks and already her thoughts were straying from her mission. It really bothered her that she could be so fickle. She *so* wanted to stay the course.

Today, as she spread paste on an eight-foot length of wallpaper, her thoughts were churning. She was relieved when the salon door opened behind her.

"Yoo-hoo, Lacy."

"Adela," she called over her shoulder, recognizing the singsong voice. "How's it going?"

"Wonderful. Just wonderful. How lovely it looks in here."

"You think so?" Paper up, Lacy stepped back, plopped her hands on her hips and admired her handiwork. "I've never hung paper before so I was excited to try something new. It's easier than I expected."

"You have the knack."

"I wouldn't say that——but it has been fairly easy."

"Have you done it all yourself?"

"Oh no, no, no. Sheri has helped big-time—she's just gone over to Pete's for more paste. I bought this paper before I left Dallas, and I didn't think about paste. Thank goodness Pete had some, but I think it had been there for a while. I hope it's still good." She spread paste on the next sheet of paper then folded it together, like the instructions said.

"I'm sure it'll be fine. It looks as if it's sticking." Adela ran a hand over the soft pink and white striped paper and nodded.

"What's up?" Lacy picked up the new length of paper and maneuvered her way to the wall.

Adela followed her. "I came to tell you that the apartments are in complete upheaval right now, but the contractor assures me that a couple of them will be ready in time for the fair. The electricians are there now, running wire for the small kitchens, and the contractors have started cutting out openings between rooms that will connect into living and dining spaces. It is amazing what can happen in a matter of days when people are motivated."

"You must have done some mighty powerful motivating." Lacy paused and smiled at Adela. Adela might have been small and serene looking, but behind that exterior, there was a very aggressive go-getter.

"I have a few connections in Ranger, great friends

of the family, and they were glad to help out, especially when they'd had another job fall through and needed to keep their men working. God has a way of clearing agendas when the time is right."

"So true, Adela."

"Lacy, I also came to tell you that we had a call a few minutes ago from a young woman who is coming out from Hollywood to see about opening a dress store. Hollywood. Can you imagine?"

Lacy spun toward Adela. "You mean to tell me you didn't come barging in here screaming with excitement about this? You amaze me, Adela! Does anything ruffle your feathers?"

Adela's eyes twinkled. "My feathers are ruffled. I'm extremely excited."

Lacy laughed. "Yeah, I can tell."

"I explained to her that at the moment a dress store might be a bit out of the question." Adela's eyes sparkled more brightly. "However we eventually expected to have a large demand for just that kind of shop."

"And," Lacy prompted when Adela frowned.

"She assured me that she expected a slow beginning. She said part of her business is done on the Internet and it really didn't matter if the foot traffic was slow in town for a little while."

"Excellent. When is she arriving?"

"In two weeks, just in time for the fair. I explained it would be the event of the summer and she would want to attend before going back to the city and making her decision."

"Adela, you are too cool," Lacy said, returning to work. The paste had set on the panel she was working on and it was time to spread the paper on the wall.

"Yes, well, thank you. Are you sure you don't need help?"

"I'm positive."

"Then I'll see you later. I'm off to see Pete about donating supplies to decorate the street. Oh, by the way, I thought the vacant building beside you would be the perfect spot for the dress shop."

"I agree," Lacy called over her shoulder, unable to spare a glance as she started working.

"Tootles, dear."

"Tootles to you, too," Lacy said absently as she smoothed the paper, concentrating on getting all the lines straight. When she finished, she backed away and surveyed her work. "Not bad. Not bad at all."

The door opened behind her.

"What do you think, Sheri? With the other paper up, this is going to look great."

"If you like pink."

Lacy swung around to find Clint Matlock frowning at the wall. She was shocked at the rush of joy that flowed over her. Shocked and dismayed at the same time.

"You don't like pink?" She willed her heart to slow

down and her mouth to smother the smile that was trying to erupt from it.

"Nope. Can't say that I do, but it's obvious we dis-
agree on the subject." He looped his thumb though the
belt loop of his right hip. "Is everything you touch
going to be pink?"

Lacy couldn't help the chuckle that bubbled out of
her. "Not everything. I like pink because it's a happy
color."

"Not always." Clint lifted his hat from his head and
slowly lowered his chin so that the top of his head was
exposed. "Like I said the other night, it's not my color."

Lacy gasped. "Clint, you have *pink hair!*"

"As if I didn't know that," he said dryly. "And it
doesn't make me happy."

Lacy hurried over to stare at his hair. "I can't believe
I didn't see this the night of the storm. But, now that I
think about it, you never once removed your hat. As a
matter of fact, I remember you yanking on it all night
to keep it in place."

"You better believe it. Since this has happened, I've
worn my hat everywhere except to bed. Do you know
what kind of teasing I'd get if word got out that I have
pink hair?"

Lacy laughed. "Oh, my, the world as we know it
would end."

Clint relaxed against the door frame. "The question
is, can you help me?"

Lacy reached up and touched the stiff patch of hair. Like the crown of a rooster's head it was a three by two section of hair sitting smack on the top of his head. It was quite cute. "You know you could just leave it and start a new trend." Clint lowered his chin and gave her that look she'd come to adore. "Okay, maybe not."

"I tried everything I thought was safe. I've showered more times than I can count. Been through a rainstorm—"

"That doesn't count," Lacy broke in. "You kept the hat on, remember." Giving into the notion, she gave the swatch of hair a gentle tug.

"Hey! Watch out."

Lacy laughed and turned away to move toward the shampoo bowl that was leaning against the back wall.

Clint followed. "I'm getting desperate enough to pour gasoline over my head. Tomorrow is Sunday and I don't usually wear my hat during services."

"I'll get it out for you." She was glad to do something for him. He had, after all, saved her from uncertain disaster. "All I need is my shampoo bowls hooked up and we're in business."

Clint eyed the equipment. "I'm handy with a wrench. I'll install the bowls if you guarantee you can make me look normal again."

Placing her hand on her heart she said somberly, "I promise."

"It's a done deal. I'll go out to my truck and get some tools, then we'll get started."

After carefully placing his Stetson back on his head and giving it a secure tug, Clint strode from the salon. Lacy watched him go, fighting laughter and the strong urge to run up behind him on the street and tip the hat off his head.

Oh, Lacy, you do have a mean streak in you.

"What's Clint up to?" Sheri asked as she came in, empty-handed.

"He's going to install my shampoo bowls."

"He's going to help you install shampoo bowls! You who crashed his Jeep, made him run his truck into a ditch, had him trudging all over his pastures in the middle of a flash flood." Her eyes were wide in disbelief.

"Yes. He's being neighborly."

"Yeah, right," Sheri snapped. "The man is interested, Lace." She thumped a fake cigar in punctuation and wiggled her eyebrows.

"Well, Groucho, I'm not." Lacy stuffed some unused wallpaper into the trash bin and ignored the kick her heart gave her ribs.

"Whatever you say, girlfriend, but I think you're crazy as a Betsy bug. Look, Pete has no more paste, so I thought I'd ride to Ranger and pick up some new paste."

"Now? Ranger is sixty miles away."

Sheri tucked her hands into her back pockets. "I know."

"Then what's up?"

"J.P. has a load of cattle to deliver to the auction barn and wanted to know if I'd ride along."

Lacy stared at her friend. "This is getting to be a pretty heavy thing between you two."

"Not too heavy. I'm holding up just fine."

"Sher—"

"Lace, stop. I'm not the one with the hang-up about men. J.P. is a very nice guy. He's fun. And, girl, can he kiss."

"Sheri, this is serious."

"Yes, it is, Lacy. You need to lighten up. That's serious. Now, while I'm gone, instead of worrying over me, why don't you worry about that handsome man who's going to be working beside you for the next hour?" Sheri backed out the door, grinning. "This is a good thing, Lacy. Remember that. A good thing. You didn't like me standing on the sidelines growing up. Well, I don't like you standing there, either. It isn't right. So loosen up and make a new friend."

Lacy watched her jog down the road to where J.P. leaned against the side of his truck. He had one leg braced against the metal fender and he looked happy watching Sheri jog up to meet him. When she came to a halt before him he wrapped an arm around her shoulders and escorted her to the truck, where he opened the door and helped her climb into the cab. A twinge of envy at their carefree attitude swept through Lacy. She turned away, shutting the emotion down. She wasn't ready yet to trust her heart to a man. Not that easily. Not that carefree. Still she envied her friend her ability to do so.

"Okay, that should do it," Clint said about an hour later. Dusting his hands off on his jeans he stood and put his wrench in his back pocket.

"Perfect," Lacy said. "That means I'm practically open for business."

"Me first."

Lacy laughed as he pulled off his hat and exposed his pink hair. "Yes, you are definitely my first client. Everybody else will have to wait until Tuesday morning."

"I have to say, you've done a great job in here. I never thought you could do it in this short time, but the place looks good. You're going to need help with those mirrors, aren't you?" He nodded toward the two large mirrors leaning against the brick wall.

"Yes, they're really heavy," Lacy admitted. She wasn't keen on more help from him. She'd become increasingly agitated working beside him installing the shampoo bowls. More times than she could count, their hands had brushed each other as she passed him tools, or held this or that for him.

"I'll hang them," he offered, interrupting her thoughts. "After—" He lowered his head and pointed at his hair.

Shrugging off her worries, Lacy smiled then dragged a shampoo chair over in front of the basin. "Sit."

"You don't have to ask me twice."

Lacy bit her lip and met his twinkling gaze, forcing herself to concentrate on getting the right stripping product out of the cabinet. The only problem was as she bent to scrub his mass of hair, he watched her. Their faces were only a few feet away from each other as she bent into the job of scrubbing. To her dismay, it took two different stripping products, and much longer than she'd hoped, to get out the paint. She was over-joyed when at last she was able to declare him paint-less. "Praise the Lord, you're a free man," she said, patting his hair down with a towel before letting him stand up.

And I'm a free woman.

Her nerves were jittering as she moved quickly away to stand by the front counter. She needed distance between them. She needed perspective on the feelings that were churning around inside her.

He crossed the room, and she watched him lean over and eye himself in the mirror. "Thank you," he said, moving toward her. "I could kiss you for this," he teased.

Lacy tapped her nails on the front counter. "We— we don't need to get carried away."

Clint took another step toward her. "If you knew how important it was to *not* have pink hair…you would understand my pleasure." He took another step toward her, mischief dancing in his eyes.

Lacy tapped her fingers harder.

"I've had you on my mind all week." His voice sombered.

They'd managed to skirt the minor problem of their emotions all afternoon and oh, how she wished he'd kept it that way. Denial was so unlike her, she who met things straight on. But this, this she was not ready to handle.

"You have?" she squeaked. Confused, thrilled.

His eyes twinkled down at her. "I'm only human. It was an eventful night."

"That is an understatement. The rain…nearly drowning, it was all so terrible." Lacy stilled her fingers and crossed her arms across her stomach.

"It wasn't all terrible, Lacy. I enjoyed being with you." He stepped up and cupped her jaw with his hand. "I enjoyed talking with you, spending time with you. You're a neat person to get to know."

Lacy closed her eyes, lost for a moment in his touch. His hand felt so gentle against her skin.

"Lace, I tried to stay away. But I can't get you off my mind."

Lacy swallowed hard and fought to gather her nerve. She couldn't allow herself this distraction. "Clint, I can't do this. I'm here to concentrate on being a witness for Christ. I would be lying if I denied wanting to get to know you better." To kiss you. "But, I can't be distracted right now. My love life is just not in the plan at the moment."

There—she had said it, or at least rattled it out. She'd been honest and straightforward. She hadn't played games with him. He deserved that much.

He studied her silently for a few moments, before his eyes sobered and his lips slashed upward into that smile of his that had the maddening habit of turning her insides to jelly.

"See you at church tomorrow."

Lacy watched Clint back out the door, then stride to his truck. She sighed. "The trouble with you, Mr. Matlock, is you're simply too cute for *my* good."

Chapter Ten

The small country church was set in a clearing on the side of town. It was a quaint beauty that had stood its ground for more than fifty years; at least that was the history that Norma had imparted to her the day before. The church was made of plank siding and sported a new metal roof that glistened in the morning sunlight. Immediately Lacy thought of an old song she faintly remembered from her childhood, about a church in the wildwood. The memory caused her heart to swell with a longing she hadn't realized was there. In Dallas, she attended a huge church of brick and stone that had every modern convenience for its members. It even had a bookstore right there inside where she could buy any Christian book she wanted. It was a wonderful church, even if you could get lost in the crowd. But as Lacy sat in her car and took in the peaceful country appearance of Mule Hollow's Church of Faith, she felt a beckoning, an almost overwhelming pull to belong. A smile overcame her as she scrambled from behind the wheel of the Caddy, refraining, in her haste, from hopping over the door—she was after all at church, and she did have on a dress. Not to mention Sheri watching her like a hawk, making certain she at least tried to act like a lady.

"Hi, Adela," she called, reaching into the back seat to pick up her Bible, waving at the same time. Adela waved back from where she was waiting on the front steps with a man whom Lacy assumed was the pastor, based on the way he was greeting everyone who entered the church. As she hurried up the walk behind Sheri, Lacy's heart hummed with excitement.

Adela hugged them when they stepped up on to the wide front porch. "I'm so happy you both made it this morning. I want to introduce you to the only man in Mule Hollow I don't think you've met. This is Pastor Lewis."

The pastor was a few inches shy of being considered tall, but he had snow-white hair and eyes so apple-green that they popped at Lacy with friendliness…or sheer joy at seeing new blood on the church premise. He took each of their hands in a firm handshake and smiled with gusto.

"You ladies don't know how long I've been praying for you to move here. The good Lord has his own timetable, but I sometimes want to get ahead of Him. But you see, when Adela told me of your coming, I could envision children playing in our playground. Children mean life, especially for church growth."

Sheri met Lacy's gaze and both women's eyes sparked with agreement.

"We're the ones who are glad to be here," Lacy said. "So far it's been cool watching things unfold." She tried not to think about Clint Matlock and the unfolding of a relationship she was baffled by with every passing day. "This church is charming," she added, pushing thoughts of Clint aside.

"Do many of the cowboys come to church?" Sheri asked, shrugging when the minister raised an eyebrow. "Sorry, I can't help myself."

Pastor Lewis chuckled. "Yes, actually quite a lot of the guys come when their work permits. Sorry to say, but sometimes a cowboy's work does not respect the Lord's Day. Here come a few more of them now. Morning, Clint and J.P. Good to see you, Bob."

Lacy turned and met Clint's gaze. She wasn't pleased at the flush she felt creep up her face. "Hello, Clint, guys." She nodded to the other cowboys that had followed Clint to the steps and now were streaming past, nodding at her and Sheri as they pulled off their hats and entered the church. Clint stood to the side after shaking hands with the pastor and Adela. Lacy heard Adela question the Pastor about the songs he wanted her to play and they excused themselves to prepare for the service. She found herself alone on the steps of the church with Clint. Sheri had eagerly gone inside with J.P. and the others.

"You look nice this morning," Clint said as he took his Stetson off and held it between both his hands. His eyes were steady as they held hers.

Lacy fought down the jitters, something which was becoming habit, and forced her traitorous voice to sound natural. "Thank you. I like your hair." You would have liked it pink!

"Why, thank you. Some really nice lady did it for me." Tension pulsed between them for a moment. Then he waved toward the door with his hat as the piano music started up. "After you."

Lacy entered the coolness of the sanctuary and was dismayed when Clint followed her into a pew. She hadn't expected to sit beside him through the service. Hiding her surprise, she reached for the songbook at the same time that he did and their hands touched. He pulled back quickly, letting her have that hymnal while he took the one beside it.

Lacy was about to give herself a good talking-to about focusing on the Lord and not Clint Matlock, when she looked into the choir and nearly bit her lip in surprise. Seeing all those singing cowboys was enough to make many a woman want to join the church, but it wasn't the cowboys that grabbed Lacy's attention. Nor were the clashing floral prints of Norma Sue and Esther Mae's Sunday dresses enough to distract her. The focus of Lacy's attention was a cute young woman. No one had mentioned a young woman in Mule Hollow.

"Who is that?" Lacy whispered to Clint, who was really getting into praising the Lord with his joyful noise.

Not that her noise was any better than his, she was just used to her own.

"Who?" he asked, bending low to hear her whisper.

"That tiny woman in the choir. That tiny *young* woman."

"Oh, that's Lilly Tipps."

"Oh."

Clint heard her confusion in her voice. "She lives on the outer edge of town, near the county line. We don't see her much except on Sundays and occasionally when she comes to town to buy feed."

"Is she married to one of the cowboys?" Lacy knew she should stop whispering in church, but she was so curious she couldn't help herself.

"Lilly. Married. Naa, it was a miracle the first time. It'll never happen a second time." Clint shook his head and resumed his singing.

Though she was still curious, especially since Lilly looked like she was in the midstage of pregnancy, Lacy squelched her questions. Instead she focused on giving praise to Lord, lifting her voice up to clash with Clint's. They sang all four stanzas of "Amazing Grace" then "Standing on the Promises". She and Clint ended grinning at each other while sharing a robust, rather off-key harmony.

When they sat down and Pastor Lewis stepped up to the pulpit, Clint leaned over and whispered, "We might not be Broadway-bound, but God has to be smiling at our effort."

"He's probably rolling with laughter." She chuckled, watching the small group of choir members file down into the congregation. Esther Mae, red hair tilting to one side, winked at them as she passed by on her way to sit with her husband. Lacy watched as Lilly Tipps moved to the far side of the sanctuary, choosing a spot on a vacant row near the side door.

Watching her, Lacy was struck by the memory of sitting beside her mother in a congregation full of people yet feeling all alone in the crowd of smiling faces. She'd always felt that her dislike of seeing people sitting on the sidelines of life stemmed from those times as a child, when she'd felt out of place in God's house. It made her all the more determined as an adult to engage others. Lacy made a mental note that Lilly Tipps would be someone she went out of her way to get to know.

The sermon was taken from 2 Peter 1:5-7 "And beside this, giving all diligence, add to your faith virtue;

and to virtue knowledge. And to knowledge temperance; and to temperance patience; and to patience godliness; And to godliness brotherly kindness; and to brotherly kindness charity."

Now Lacy could have believed that the pastor had read her diary, if she kept a diary. The sermon was so close to her heart. It was very thought provoking for her, because if she wanted to work for the Lord she had to learn control…and that was in all aspects of her life.

Beside her, Clint shifted in his seat and drew her attention. Her manner with him was very upsetting to her. He was one of the first people she'd met coming to Mule Hollow, and constantly she lost it with him. He'd very nearly saved her life, and she had treated him terrible half the time. Of course, part of that was because of the maddening attraction she had toward him. God's sense of humor once again. Here she was struggling with issues while new issues kept being thrown her way. Of course, she *had* always been told never to pray for patience without being prepared for war.

When the service ended, Lacy felt determined, with God's help, to overcome her loose lips. It could be done; she just needed, as Pastor Lewis had pointed out, to rely more fully on His lead rather than her own.

Which was exactly what Lacy was striving to do.

To Lacy's disappointment, Lilly Tipps left quickly though the side door and was nowhere to be seen when

Lacy made it outside. Lacy had hoped to meet her and make a new friend.

"Lacy," Sheri said, coming up with J.P. as Lacy made her way to the car, after having said her good-byes, "I'm going on a picnic with J.P. Want to come?"

The last thing Lacy wanted was to be the third wheel. "No, thanks. All I want is to go home and crash for a while, maybe read a book. But the two of you have fun."

Sheri hugged her, and then headed toward J.P.'s truck as happy as a schoolgirl. The country life was agreeing with Sheri and that was good. Although Lacy had to admit that she missed her friend's company. Since coming to Mule Hollow they really saw less of each other than when they lived in Dallas. It was funny how she felt more alone in this small town than she had in the Metroplex.

"Hey, Lacy, wait up."

Lacy had just reached her car. Turning around, she faced Clint as he came up beside her.

"Are you being stood up for the afternoon?"

"You could say that," she said, and fought to keep her voice from betraying her lonesome mood.

"Are you okay? You sound a little down."

So much for keeping her chin up. "I'm just think-ing. That's all."

Clint ducked his chin and searched her eyes thoughtfully. "Well, look, I owe you for saving Flossy's calf the other day and thought maybe I could feed you lunch."

"You don't owe me. You saved me from the storm the other night and you installed my shampoo bowls. Math isn't my strong point, but by my calculations I think we're even on that score."

"I thought you wanted to see Junior?"

He had her on that one. She smiled. "I do want to see the baby. He's doing good, right?" The offer was tempting.

"Getting fatter as we speak. Come on back to the ranch with me, and after I throw a couple of steaks on the pit, we'll go see the little guy. I promise to keep my hands to myself, if that's what's worrying you."

Lacy's heart lifted and she laughed. "In that case, you're on, cowboy."

Clint watched Lacy as she tickled the white curly forehead of the rowdy calf. Her blue eyes sparkled with genuine glee as Junior nudged and prodded her hand with his wet nose.

Clint was leaning against the stall gate and lost his breath when Lacy turned those glittering eyes toward him. Just as their gazes connected, Junior butted her in the ribs and knocked her to the hay-strewn floor. Most women would have screamed, but Lacy busted out laughing, while he hurried to pull the overzealous calf off her.

"I told you he was feeling good," he said, reaching down and taking her hand while he held the calf back with the other hand.

"You were right," she said breathlessly between chuckles, accepting his outstretched hand. "I'm so glad he's doing well."

The baby nudged Lacy roughly in the hip. "I think he has a crush on you," Clint said, grinning. "Come on, let's get you out of here before you get hurt."

Pulling her through the gate, he closed it quickly so that Junior couldn't follow. The sound of Lacy's laughter washed over Clint like sunshine breaking through cloud-filled sky. He was drawn to her by something he'd never felt before. And though buried in his desk drawer he had a reminder of all the reasons he should walk away from her, he couldn't.

"What did you do to that baby?" she asked. They'd started walking toward the house their arms brushing as they walked. "He's as strong as an ox."

"It's nothing I did. He just knows a pretty lady when he sees one."

"Flattery, Mr. Matlock?" she asked with a sideways glance. Her soft white hair sparkled in the sun and her white teeth flashed at him against her golden skin.

"Hey, I just tell it like it is, Miss Brown. I see your sunburn is turning to a tan. I was afraid you were going to be a peeling mess."

"Me, too. But I usually tan unless I'm foolish and

really overdo it. Thanks to you, I escaped the sun just in time." She stopped walking and placed her hand on his forearm. "Really, thanks for coming to my rescue. Again."

Clint squeezed her hand and then led her along a flagstone pathway around the corner of his ranch house to a private deck that stretched out from the back of the house over a sloping hillside. The view was breathtaking. Clint's land flowed beyond the deck's railing like a patchwork of greens dotted with brown and black cattle and the blues of a stream dissecting the pastures in a lazy arch.

"Oh, Clint. What a treasure," she gasped.

He stepped up onto the deck and pulled out a chair at the patio table for her. He'd worked hard on his home and it was nice to hear someone admire it.

"My dad picked this home site forty years ago." Since his father's death, Clint had done a number of renovations to the place and he appreciated his father's choice of building site even more, now that he'd done so much of the work himself.

Lacy accepted the willow chair he offered.

"This is interesting looking," she said, running her hands over the tabletop. "What kind of wood is this?"

"It's mesquite."

"You mean those awful scrub trees?"

"The same." Clint moved to the huge grill and the steaks he had waiting to cook.

"Who would have ever believed you could make something so beautiful with something so—"

"Useless," Clint finished for her.

"Exactly. Another reminder of how everything God created has beauty. Sometimes it simply takes sanding and polishing to make it gleam."

Clint smiled. That was Lacy, always seeing the big picture. He continued to work at the stone counter.

"Here let me do something," Lacy said, joining him. "I can help. Really."

"Okay, you can go into the kitchen and bring out the salad. It's in the fridge. Can you grab the tray with the cheese and butter for the potatoes too?"

"Sure thing, I'll be right back."

He watched her bound into the house, happy as a lark. He'd had a hard time sitting beside her in church earlier. She couldn't carry a note any better than he could, but they'd praised the Lord with smiles on their faces and joy in their hearts. Sharing that kind of worship had been an unbelievable experience. It was also cause for concern on his part. He'd started seeing Lacy in a better light than he had when she'd first come to town. Still, he had reservations about his feelings for her.

Thoughts of the letter gathering dust in the drawer in his office reminded him that things could change in the blink of an eye. His mother had once seemed to love the Lord, too.

Pushing aside thoughts of the letter from his mother, determined to give Lacy a chance, he forced himself to look at all the good Lacy had done since coming to Mule Hollow.

Despite his reservations, he'd begun to believe that the town might just benefit from her ideas and energy. He'd noticed during the sermon that she'd grown very thoughtful and he wondered if something in the message had bothered her.

"Wow," she said, coming out of the French doors, her arms loaded down. "Your house looks like it came straight off the showcase floor of a building center."

"Thanks. A lot of labor went into those rooms."

"I can tell." She set the salads down and arranged the condiments.

"Lacy, may I ask you something?" He turned to face her. Folding his arms across his chest, he leaned against the rock counter.

"Sure, anything."

"Was something bothering you this morning during the service? I'd like to help."

For a moment her eyes registered uncertainty before she looked away.

"I'm feeling a little confused, is all."

"I'm a good listener."

She took a deep breath and toyed with a napkin, laid it aside then tapped her purple fingernail on the table in her familiar impatient fashion. "Okay, here it is." She strode to the deck railing and looked out over the landscape. The gentle breeze ruffled her hair as she turned to face him. "You know what a mouth I have on me. Not cursing or anything like that, but just a big mouth… I'm sure you haven't noticed that."

Clint laughed at that. "Maybe a little."

She made a funny face at him, then started pacing. Clint enjoyed watching her. She had on a soft dress that, like the dress she wore the night of the flood, swirled around her calves as she moved. Her face was animated as she spun to face him.

"I'm going to be nicer from here on out. "

"Does that mean things are going to be boring now?" He was disappointed that she might change. Surprising, but true. He took steaks off the grill, plopped their foil-covered baked potatoes on the plates and took them to the table.

Lacy followed him to her seat at the table. "With me around… Are you kidding?"

"Lacy Brown, I have an idea that it will never be boring anywhere within a two-day drive from where you are."

Lacy laughed. "I hope that's a good thing."

"A very good thing." He couldn't help wonder what he was getting himself into by becoming friends with Lacy.

"But." Lacy grew thoughtful. "Oh, how I would love to tame my mouth."

He concentrated on adding cheese and butter to his potato then paused. "Do you really think your outspokenness is all that bad?"

Lacy stopped preparing her potato. "Maybe."

"Hold that thought while I say the prayer." They bowed their heads and he thanked God for the food and good company. "So let me get this straight. God Himself doesn't like it?" He took a bite of his steak and watched her contemplate his question. Man, she was cute when she thought really hard. She had reminded him of Meg Ryan the first time he saw her, but when she put her thinking cap on, she really had similar facial expressions. It was entertaining just watching the metamorphosis.

"Not exactly." She pointed her fork at him and smiled. "You sure you want to hear my exhortation on how I don't measure up?"

"Yes, I do." She was serious. The carefree Lacy Brown actually thought she wasn't good enough. The idea slammed into Clint. It wasn't anything like what he expected her to feel. She came across so in tune with herself.

"Well, that list could go on forever. Let's just say that I feel pretty defeated every time my exuberance leads me down the wrong path. Oh, how I wish I could think before I act or speak, more often."

"I have a feeling God likes watching your exuberance. I know I do." He said it and he knew it was true. Who couldn't enjoy watching someone as full of life as Lacy? Who couldn't want to be that way themselves? "You're pretty funny, Lacy Brown."

"You're pretty funny yourself." She grinned as she cut into her steak.

"My dad taught me." Clint cut his steak and let the memories of his dad fill his mind.

"He must have been a wonderful man."

Clint smiled. "The best. A kid couldn't have asked to be loved by a dad any more than I was. Not that we didn't have our differences, but even though—" Clint paused, his heart ached for a moment. He was weirdly emotional today. His feelings seemed to be crowding in on him. "Even though he didn't always tell me he loved me, I knew it."

Lacy put down her fork and laid her small hand over his. "A kid can tell these things. Love is an emotion that doesn't always need words." She squeezed his hand, then pulled back, fiddling with her napkin before picking up her fork again. "I see it all the time in my salon. People, especially men, talking about their kids, and though they don't just blurt out, *'I love my kid'*, it's in the things they say, the way they express themselves. It's in their eyes."

Her eyes held his. Clint could listen to her talk forever.

She leaned her head to the side and smiled. "My mom was different. She told me she loved me almost every hour. I think it had to do with my dad leaving. I think she wanted to reassure me that her love would always be there for me. But she didn't have to worry about that. I knew."

"Where is your mom now?"

"She remarried and moved to Okalahoma. She's very happy. She was excited about me coming to Mule Hollow."

"Really. She wasn't worried about you?"

"Maybe, but if she was, she wouldn't tell me. She got used to my weird ways a long time ago."

Clint thought about that for a moment.

"You make a killer steak." Lacy beamed. "This is really good."

Clint put his fears aside, refusing to dim the wonderful afternoon he was having. "You keep being nice and I might tell you my secret sometime." He was glad to change the subject. He was only human, and he enjoyed her playfulness.

"You tell me your secret and I'll tell you my secret to the best berry cobbler in the world."

Clint leaned back in his chair, folded his arms behind his head and stretched. "Berry cobbler, huh? Let me think about this. You can actually cook. A cobbler?"

"Weird but true."

"You might have to prove that to me before I give you my secrets."

"You've got a deal, cowboy."

Chapter Eleven

Tangled in her daisy-dotted sheets, Lacy plopped over onto her back as the Monday-morning sunshine crept through her bedroom window. It was the first day of a new week. "Good morning, Lord," she said, stretching like a kitten in a sunbeam. Rubbing her eyes with her fist, she sat up. Swinging her legs over the side of the bed, she swung them sideways for a few seconds. She loved mornings. Padding to the bathroom, she brushed her teeth, ran some water through her wild natural waves then picked up her Bible and walked into the kitchen.

Her morning coffee sat waiting and ready for her, thanks to a nifty coffeemaker. After filling her mug she walked out onto the porch and curled up in the swing with God's word.

She'd started sitting in the swing soon after she and Sheri moved into their little cottage. She felt wonderful today. She knew it was because of her afternoon with Clint the day before. "Father, he said he enjoyed my exuberance." She spoke aloud as she thumbed through the Bible. Clint had reminded her before she came home that Peter held a special place in God's heart. In doing so he'd given her something to think about. But this morning she paused in her Bible study, her thoughts fixed on Clint.

She wondered what had happened to his mom after she'd abandoned him. She wondered how he felt toward his mom. Did he ever see her? Had he forgiven her?

It was a huge question Lacy understood completely. She had forgiven her dad for casting her aside for another life. Lacy looked out over the backyard lost in thought. After her dad walked out, she'd never seen him again. It had taken a long time to understand that she needed to forgive her father even if she couldn't see him face-to-face. Even if he hadn't asked to be forgiven. Or cared.

She couldn't help feeling that maybe Clint needed to come to terms with some form of reconciliation with his mother.

She might not have known the love of an earthly dad but she had the all-encompassing love of an awesome heavenly Father.

Lacy and Sheri arrived at Adela's for a planning session and a walk through of Mule Hollow's newly opened apartments-slash-bed-and-breakfast.

The old Howard estate had been built in 1904 by Adela's grandfather on her mother's side. Originally built as a boardinghouse, it thrilled Adela that she was able to bring it full circle. There were six small one-bedroom apartments. There were also two bedrooms that Adela left for bed-and-breakfast rooms for those who were just staying a short time. The house had a huge kitchen and dining room, and though Adela and her husband had raised their three children in the house, the upkeep had been far too much for her after her children moved on and her husband died. She had lived next door in a small cottage for the past ten years. Today there were tears in her eyes when she greeted Lacy and Sheri at the door.

Lacy lost her breath when she and Sheri stepped through the door. The woodwork was gleaming and the dark hardwood floors shone. The staircase that rose three stories was magnificent as it wound upward from the entrance hall.

"Adela, this is fabulous," Sheri actually exclaimed before Lacy could get her breath.

"Oh, Adela," Lacy gasped. "What a treasure this is."

"Come in," Adela invited, breathless with pleasure. "I'm so thrilled with the outcome that I could quite literally burst. My granddaddy would be so pleased that his home was about to be lived in and admired again. You know he did much of the carving himself."

They followed her through the large rooms with its

era furniture and crisp white curtains. The home was filled with ornate crushed velvet couches that invited one to sit and read a book. Lacy could envision the place packed with people. The bookcases were even packed with books that had probably been collected over one hundred years. What a treasure.

In the kitchen, Norma Sue and Esther Mae were polishing silverware. Their chatter filled the house, and Lacy laughed as they drew close.

"With all this standing we're going to be doing I bought me some of those Neutralizer shoes to wear," Esther Mae was saying as Lacy stepped into the kitchen. "They are supposed to be real good for your feet if you're standing all day."

Norma Sue paused in her spoon rubbing. "That's *Naturalizers,* Esther Mae."

"Oh, well, either way they are comfortable. My feet feel like they are floating on air. And look, ya'll—" she lifted her hefty leg up "—they're cute, too. Lacy, you need to get you a pair of these for standing on your feet all day in the salon."

"I might try me some. Thanks for the advice." Lacy pulled out a stool and sat down at the bar.

"Just make sure you buy the *Naturalizers* and not the *Neutralizers,*" piped in Norma Sue. "Unless of course you have a bad case of foot odor!"

Everybody got tickled at that, and Esther Mae turned as red as her hair.

While Lacy joined in on the silver polishing, Adela and Sheri fixed a plate of sandwiches and iced tea. When they carried the food to the table, everyone sat down, joined hands and prayed for the food and the town.

"I have a surprise to share," Adela said as they passed the platter around. "Three apartments are spoken for and the two guest rooms are booked for the weekend of the fair."

"Hallelujah!" exclaimed Norma Sue.

"Sheri, I told you they would come." Lacy beamed, reaching out to accept the hug Sheri offered.

"I hoped you would be right," she said, grinning.

Esther Mae patted her updo and expelled a long breath. "Whew, I can hardly wait. When are they coming?"

"Let's see, Ashby Templeton is coming out from California at the end of next week. She's the one interested in opening a dress store. She said she had grown weary of the city and has been looking for a place to open a store. She has a Web site that she sells her clothing on and does a very good business there. So she is a perfect candidate."

Everyone exchanged thrilled smiles, then waited for Adela to continue.

"Two of the apartments are being rented by schoolteachers. We had very good timing with the ad, because a lot of the new teachers coming into the school system hadn't relocated to the area yet, and decided to give us a chance. And then the last room is a columnist and freelance reporter for the *Houston Times*. Her name is Molly Popp. Isn't that a cute name? Reminds me of that old song about lollipops. She said she did a lot of traveling, but was tired and had really been thinking about settling down and writing a book. She is renting a room, but if she feels this is a place she would like to stay, then she is going to rent an apartment. Can you imagine, ladies, she might settle here also?"

Everyone was clapping and she waved them silent. "But it gets better. She's mentioning the fair in her weekly column, and encouraging single women and even families to come out to participate in it. *Then* she's writing an article about the fair's success."

Lacy's heart pounded in her chest as she closed her eyes and thanked God for His faithfulness. Mule Hollow wasn't going to be a sad little town anymore. This was only the beginning.

By Wednesday, Adela had sent out the word that help was needed, and now the entire population of Mule Hollow was standing on Main Street ready to work.

If people were coming, and it sounded like they were, then the ladies wanted them to stay. That meant Mule Hollow had to greet them with more than a sad sigh. It needed to grab their attention and invite them to put down roots from the moment they entered. The ladies and Lacy had decided it was time to put out the call and paint the entire town.

Lacy was impressed. When Adela spoke, people listened. Every rancher and cowboy within twenty miles had to be standing in front of her holding a paint-brush. Why, every parking space along the street had a vehicle in it!

And Clint was one of those who'd shown up.

He'd come bright and early with a trail of black pickups following him. He had helped her organize the tables and cans of paint that Pete had sold them at rock-bottom prices. And now it was time to expose her plan and open the paint.

"Now, all you boys don't get disturbed when I start pulling off these lids." Lacy looked around the crowd, a gleam in her eye then she pried the first lid off a can of canary-yellow paint. All the masculine faces went slack, but she still had them. Then she ripped off the lid of a can of deep raspberry, and they all took a step back.

"Now, don't go anywhere. I promise these colors will be perfect." She could tell they didn't believe her. Clint stood to the side of the group with his Stetson pulled low and his arms crossed over his chest. The hat cast a shadow over his eyes but she could see the half grin of his full lips. Encouraged, she popped the tops off a few more cans.

"Miss Lacy, are we really supposed to paint these buildings those colors?" someone asked.

"Yes, we are." Lacy stood and slowly met each cowboy's gaze, challenging them to believe. "I'm promising you this will work. This is going to be the happiest town in Texas. When people get within nine miles of this place, they're going to see us on the horizon."

"That's for sure," someone else said, igniting laughter. Lacy smiled; she'd expected this.

"Look at my building. I bet when I started painting it everyone didn't think it would look as good as it does now." No one said anything. "Okay," she said, thinking, "in Texas, on a long flat stretch of road between Houston and Huntsville, there's this section of road about nine miles long, and in honor of General Sam Houston, there stands a gigantic statue of him at the entrance of the state park. It has only been there for a few years, and before it was constructed, that long lane of highway was one boring drive.

"For people traveling that stretch of road for the first time it seemed endless, especially if there were kids. Then someone got the idea of constructing this beautiful tribute there." She had started moving among the guys as she talked. "He's huge." She waved her arms wide. Everyone was listening. "Now, when people come over that hill and hit that long, long stretch they see a white spot at the end of the road before it disappears around a bend. *A white spot.*" She stopped and put her hands on her hips. "I know, I know, what does a white spot change, you ask? Honestly, not much. But there is this *spot* and people are driving and they are squinting and they are saying, What is that? *What. is that?* And as they drive, they become so engrossed in wondering what's on the horizon, well, the miles just roll by."

She had come full circle now and was back beside the paint cans. "And as they draw closer, the white spot starts taking shape and soon there he is. General Sam Houston himself, and looking at him is so cool. He even has a wart on his nose. Many people who would have passed on by stop and get out of their cars and look at the monument. Now what does that have to do with us, with Mule Hollow? Everything. What did you used to see when you hit the five-mile mark outside of town?"

"Some ugly brown buildings," Clint said, pushing back his Stetson.

Lacy nodded, beaming. "Yep, yep, yep. Boring brown wood. Now what do you see?"

"Well, it sure ain't nothing white," J.P. said with a grin. "But I kinda like seein' your pink building popping out at me like a big surprise. I've kinda started looking forward to it."

"You do? I mean, *yes*. That's what I mean." Lacy was ecstatic when all the guys started nodding and voicing agreement with J.P. When Clint caught the edge of his hat and tipped it to her, her heart started thumping harder. "Okay," she said to the group, "so now we paint."

She was busy after that splitting the fellas into groups of two and three, showing them how appealing each colored building would be with the right trim and adornment. The vision God had given her was there and it thrilled her when everyone seemed to warm to it.

Right before they broke into their groups, she was as thrilled as the cowboys, when Sam's niece Amy drove in to town from San Angelo with a carload of girlfriends. College students wanted every opportunity to be around a bunch of hunks, as she put it to Lacy a few minutes after they climbed out of their car.

Clint was heading up the replacement of sidewalk planks and broken windows. And Lacy found herself pausing her painting to watch him in action.

He was quite handy with a saw and a hammer. Norma Sue had suggested he be appointed head of the carpentry duties, after telling Lacy that he had practically renovated his ranch house all by himself.

Lacy had been impressed with the beauty of his home. She wondered why he hadn't told her he'd done the work. She had commented on certain things while she was there, like the massive tiled outdoor kitchen that surrounded the patio where they had eaten lunch. Norma told her that he had just finished that project last winter. It made sense; a cowboy needed something to do after dark on a winter night. He was humble, and though it looked like a talented professional had done the work, Clint had kept that to himself.

Lacy went back to painting, liking the raspberry paint she was applying to the building next to her salon. She kept having to remind herself more and more that she hadn't come to Mule Hollow to think about Clint Matlock. But every so often she would catch him watching her, and when she happened to catch him at it, he would tip his hat at her again, and turn those lips into a slow smile that seemed to light a path right up to her feet.

It was really hard not to think about that, and get lost in her confusion. But she forced herself to have fun like everyone else seemed to be having. It was almost like a fair day without the planning.

Adela and Esther Mae served colas, sandwiches and chicken all through the day, while Norma Sue supplied paint refills to anyone whose paint trays started drying up. Pete, a robust man with a quick smile, stood around and told jokes to anyone who would listen as he watched his old weather-beaten building become a bright grass-green, trimmed in daffodil-yellow. And when it was complete, that's when Lacy got excited. It looked awesome. It looked fantastic! It looked just the way she had envisioned it that first morning when she'd surveyed her new home from the seat of her Caddy.

Best of all, the bright paint brought excitement to the dusty streets of Mule Hollow. The college girls commented on how much fun they were having and how much nicer the painted buildings made the town.

And no one complained about the colors anymore. Everyone had started to see "her vision" as they'd begun to call it. She kept explaining to each person who would listen that it was God's vision.

Clint guided his horse over the dry riverbed and up the bank onto the other side of the ravine. He'd neglected his ranch for three days, while he and his ranch hands had helped paint the town.

Now he was checking back pastures for tire tracks and broken fence line. He'd also come to the more remote area of his ranch to think.

He couldn't deny the enjoyment he'd gotten watching Lacy Brown in action. The woman was something. She had ramrodded the painting of the town with such excitement that every skeptic had begun to believe in what she wanted to accomplish.

The transformation Main Street had gone through in three days was amazing. Once sad and ghostlike, the town was now bright and inviting. She had instructed him to build window boxes for second-story windows, and she'd filled them to overflowing with lively silk flowers. Getting into the swing of things, Clint had taken a few hours, nailed together some planks, and now Sam's Place and Pete's had picnic tables sitting out front. There were even tablecloths and flowers adorning the ones outside of Sam's.

He chuckled, remembering the looks on all the guy's faces when she'd started popping off can tops to expose the colors. For a moment he'd thought everyone was going to turn and run. But Lacy had calmed them down and talked them into going along with her ideas.

One look into those sparkling eyes and he'd been hooked. Despite his trepidation about her in the beginning, he was starting to think using his mother as a yardstick to judge Lacy by had been wrong. Lacy's sincerity exploded from her with everything she did. Her worries about God wanting her to tame her tongue tickled him. And touched him. For her to be concerned about being the right kind of woman in a world filled with excuses for everything…well, that spoke volumes for her character.

Clint brought his horse to a halt at the edge of a ravine overlooking a huge portion of his ranch. As far as he could see, he owned the land. He was thirty-five years old and tired. Tired of working all day and going home to a silent house. Tired of working on projects for his home when there was no one to share it with. He was tired of having his king-size bed all to himself. What good did everything he owned do him, when there was no one to share it with and no child to leave it to?

His mother had run away with the owner of a small-time circus that had camped out on the outskirts of Mule Hollow for the winter. Clint had only been eight but he'd been old enough to know his mother wasn't happy. There had been a time when she was so high on life that all they did was laugh at home. And then something had changed around the time the town started dying and people moved away.

Many of his mother's friends were forced to leave, and with his dad always working on the ranch, she'd become lonely. He hadn't understood everything then, but over the years the understanding came to him. She'd been lonely, and the owner of the circus had offered a diversion. His dad had tried not to let Clint blame her, by taking on most of the blame himself for having neglected her.

The letter he'd refused to open tugged at his conscience. He pushed the thought away and directed his horse to start the treacherous path down into the valley. His mother's betrayal had devastated his dad, who had thrown himself into his work in order to live through the pain. That had become their way of life.

It had been fifteen years since his dad's death, and Clint had carried on his legacy. Work, work and more work. Until Lacy Brown had blasted into his life, he hadn't known how much he wanted more.

But the more he thought about her, the more he wondered. What if this was simply a phase Lacy was going through? What if she grew bored with Mule Hollow?

What if he fell in love with her before she left?

Chapter Twelve

"Okay, are you reaaaddddy to rummmbbbble?" Lacy asked Esther Mae as they stared at each other's reflections in the mirror. Lacy held her scissors right above a lock of red hair. Behind them Norma Sue, Adela and Sheri watched expectantly.

Esther Mae squeezed her eyes shut and nodded her head. "It's now or never. Let's do it."

That was all the encouragement Lacy needed. With one quick motion she sliced through the hair and tossed it over her shoulder. "How'd that feel?"

Esther grinned, "Like a relief. More please. I can't wait to see the new me."

"Anything would be an improvement," Norma Sue yelled, from under the dryer, not realizing she was yelling. She was sitting half under the hood with a bag over her head and one ear turned their way so she wouldn't miss any of the conversation.

"Your hair will look wonderful shorter," Adela said calmly from the manicure table where Sheri was pampering her hands with a paraffin treatment.

The music was playing and Lacy was happily snipping away. The only picture of what Esther Mae was going to look like was in her creative mind's eye. Having fun with it, she continued to toss hair over her shoulder as she cut, thrilled to be open for business and that Esther's red bird's nest was Heavenly Inspirations' first casualty.

Everything was coming together for the fair day, and now that her salon was open for business, she felt great.

"We're almost there, Esther. Just a few more snips and you'll be able to wash and go."

"Am I going to be as good a makeover as Main Street was?"

"*Nothing can compare to Main Street,*" yelled Norma Sue from beneath the hair drier.

"She's going to break our eardrums." Adela chuckled.

"*What?*" Norma Sue barked and, everyone burst out laughing. Norma raised an eyebrow and lifted the hood. "What's so funny?"

"You," Esther snapped. "You're screaming."

"Oh—" Norma laughed "—can you tell I'm not used to this sort of thing?"

"It's not just you, Norma," Lacy said. "A lot of people do the same thing. And now that I'm here, this is going to become like a second home to you. I'm going to pamper you all the time. Okay, Esther, let's blow-dry and we're done."

A few minutes later everyone was speechless.

"Wow," Esther Mae gasped. "Who is that?"

Lacy smiled proudly. Esther's huge hair was gone and in its place was a softly curling short cut that swept away from her face on both sides in a gentle wave. Her cheek bones seemed to lift off her plump face, creating hollows that hadn't been there before. Her eyebrows were just exposed by a soft wisp of a half bang creating an updated and casual new look.

Everyone finally found their voices and let Esther Mae know how wonderful she looked. Lacy felt a satisfaction deep inside, and once again she knew this was a career she could love for a lifetime.

"Okay, so when is it my turn?" asked Norma.

"Right now. Let's rinse out this conditioner, and then we'll get started."

"Do you have any idea what to do with this stuff?"

Lacy started rinsing out the conditioner. "Yes, I do. I've been thinking about how to fix your hair since the first time I saw you."

"Is that so?"

"Yup, that's so. Now come over to the hot seat." Norma hurried over and hopped into the chair. Her kinky hair was all spiked. Lacy started combing.

"While I do this, let's talk about what else we need to do to get this fair day off the ground."

"I'm supposed to take flyers to Ranger tomorrow," Sheri offered. "J.P. is going with me."

"Good. Make sure you put them all over the place," Norma said. "Lacy, are you cutting all my hair off?"

"No, Norma, just half of it. Relax, would you?"

"Clint is going to supply the hay for the seating," Adela said, intent on picking out a nail polish. "Lacy, have any of the men been in for haircuts?"

Lacy shook her head. "They think this is a *beauty parlor.* I'll have to do some convincing to get the guys in here. When you talk to them about coming here, please refer to it as the *salon.*"

"When are some of the boarders coming?" Esther asked as Sheri helped her dip her hands into the paraffin.

Adela looked up from polish picking. "Some will be here Saturday for the fair."

"I certainly hope we have a good turnout," Esther said.

"We will have a great turnout." Lacy spun around and faced everyone. "Think positive."

"Now, we are clear on what games we are going to play, right?" Norma asked, eyeing her vanishing hair with a worried expression.

"Yup." Lacy smiled and kept on cutting. "Horse-shoes, washers, watermelon seed spitting, the three-legged race, cow chip toss—"

"Cow *what* toss?" Sheri asked, looking appalled.

"You heard right." Lacy laughed. "With all these dried cow patties, why shouldn't we have a Texas Frisbee-throwing contest?"

"For starters, it's gross!"

"Sheri, you are going to toss one and I'm going to toss two or three. It'll be great fun."

"I'm tossin' one, too," Esther Mae said.

"Okay, Norma Sue," Lacy said, picking up a bottle of leave-in conditioner. She squirted a little in her palm then rubbed it through Norma's hair. "This is a must-have for your wiry curl. I've textured the curls so that with just a little of the moisturizer you should have an entirely different feeling to your hair. There, what do you think?"

Norma blinked. "How'd you do that? Look, ya'll, my curls are soft. Lacy Brown, I love you."

"Knock, knock." Everyone turned to find Clint peeking in the doorway. "Is this a private party? Or can a cowboy get a haircut?"

"I'd love to give a cowboy a haircut," Lacy said. She was so glad to see Clint. "Come in. I was just finishing with Norma. What do you think?"

Clint placed his hat on the rack next to the door and strode into the room. "Goodness, Norma, you look great."

He circled the beaming Norma, and Lacy enjoyed watching the way she blushed. Lacy knew that Clint and Norma had a close relationship and she enjoyed watching them together.

"You think Roy Don will like it?" she asked, patting her soft curls.

"Like it. Yeah, he's going to like it. Make him take you out on the town. Not our town. Make him take you to a nice restaurant in Ranger. Whoa…" He whistled as he glimpsed Esther Mae. "Lacy, you are good. Esther, you look spiffy. Ya'll better make it a double date."

The ladies laughed and patted their new hairstyles.

Esther spun to look at Norma. "We could go try out that new steak house in Ranger. You know, the Texas Roadkill, or something like that."

"It's the Texas Road House. They have something named after roadkill on the menu," Norma said. "But I heard it was real good. Come on, let's go snag our boys and head that way. Adela, do you want to come? We could grab Sam. That man probably hasn't been out of the county in decades."

Adela looked thoughtful for a moment. "You know, I bet you're right. It would do Sam good to get out from behind that counter of his."

Lacy and Clint exchanged hidden smiles as Adela stood up and smoothed her dainty dress.

"I think I'll go over and invite Sam to come along."

"Atta girl, Miss Adela," Clint said, holding the door open for the ladies. They strolled out onto the sidewalk shoulders back, heads up. "You all have a good time. And remember your curfews."

"Clint Matlock," Esther Mae said, wagging a finger at him, "you mind your own business. We just might not come home till the rooster crows."

Everybody chuckled then practically bounced down the sidewalk chattering excitedly.

"Lacy—" Sheri sighed "—see what we did. That makes me glad I followed you on this adventure."

"Yep, and I'm glad you came, too, 'cause if I had to paint those nails, they wouldn't be too happy right now."

"That's the awful truth." Sheri laughed, turning to remove her smock.

Clint closed the door and looked from one to the other of them. "What does that mean?"

Sheri turned back and walked toward the door. "Only that Lacy is really good with hair, but she literally can't paint the broad side of a barn, much less a fingernail."

Lacy shrugged. "It's true. I make a mess just thinking about nail polish."

Clint relaxed against the counter, next to the small cash register. "But I thought they taught you those things at school."

"Oh, they try," Lacy said, widening her eyes. "But some things have to come naturally. And just because they teach both at beauty school doesn't mean a person will have talent in both."

Sheri was looking out the window. "That's why we make a great team. We both appreciate what the other does. Oh, there's my ride. Catch ya later."

The room was suddenly silent as the door slammed shut behind Sheri.

"Wow, I can really clean out a joint. Is it something I said?" Clint asked.

"Naa, it wasn't you. They were all just excited. And Sheri had already said she was going with J.P. again to do something." It was obvious to Lacy that everyone wanted her and Clint to be alone together. Who was she kidding? She wanted to be alone with Clint. She had enjoyed their lunch on Sunday. And that had nearly been a week ago. Though she'd seen him every day that they worked on the town, they hadn't had the chance to really talk a lot. His being here in the salon reminded her of the last time he'd been here with his pink hair, and suddenly her mouth went dry.

"Looks like you've been busy."

Lacy looked at all the hair on the floor and reached for the broom. She needed something to distract her. "I have. It felt wonderful. I wanted the gals to be my first clients, so I could pamper them a bit. I've wanted to do that for Norma and Esther from the moment I met them."

Clint was studying her as she dumped the dustpan full of hair into the garbage. He seemed to be evaluating something.

"Is everything okay?" she asked, turning back to him while squelching the jitters that threatened to overcome her.

"Everything's…good."

He ran a hand through his hair, a habit that she'd come to associate with him almost as much as the thumb-to-the-hat trick. However, his eyes were downcast and that was something she didn't associate with him at all. "For some reason, I don't believe you. If…you need a friend to talk to, hairdressers make great listeners."

He smiled that slow smile of his and lifted that lean chin just enough for her to see those eyes. Her heart skipped a few beats. Quickly she turned away and walked to the shampoo bowl hoping to calm her nerves. "Come over here and let me give you a shampooing. You know the routine. Nothing relaxes someone like a great shampoo."

"I kind of like the shampoo part," he said, smiling that killer smile as he sat down and leaned his head back.

Lacy's hands were trembling before she even touched his thick dark hair. Thank goodness he couldn't see them.

"That was nice of you to want to do something special for Norma and Esther. They're good women, and out here in this forsaken backwoods, there isn't anywhere for a woman to be pampered."

He was watching her closely and she paused in her vigorous scalp massage. "That's one of the reasons I'm so glad I'm here. God gave me a vision for witnessing to the women that are going to come to Mule Hollow. But Norma, Esther and Adela who, by the way, only had her nails done today because her hair is already perfect—anyway, I love doing things for them." Lacy found herself staring down at Clint and smiling. Hastily she busied herself with finishing his shampoo then led him to her chair.

He continued to silently watch her in the mirror as she started combing his wet locks. He looked as uncomfortable as she felt. Trying not to be a klutz, she picked up her scissors and began to trim his hair. Touching him was hard enough—her insides kept getting all fluttery feeling, and his watching her so intently didn't help the situation. She wanted to pursue the reason for his somberness but couldn't. If she opened her mouth she might start talking nonstop because of her nervousness. What a hoot! She was afraid of what she might say.

When Clint did speak, it startled her because she was concentrating so intently on ignoring the feelings that were swirling around inside of her.

"What are you going to do when you move on from Mule Hollow?" His voice was gruff.

She had just folded his ear down to trim the crease hidden there and she paused. "Move on? What do you mean?"

"Lacy, you're ambitious and obviously very talented, judging by what I saw this afternoon. Why would you want to stay in a hole-in-the-road town like Mule Hollow? I mean even if this plan works and we are able to get some life back into the town, it still won't have much to offer you."

The edge in his voice bothered Lacy. She hadn't heard it before and it sent warning signals to her heart. There was more to the question than was being asked.

"Consider Proverbs 27:8, Clint, 'As a bird wandereth from her nest, so is a man that wandereth from his place.'"

Lacy remembered the verse God had led her to that morning in her Bible study. And she understood. God had touched her when she read it.

"I won't be leaving Mule Hollow. I feel as if I've found my place, my nest. I feel like Mule Hollow is the home I've been looking for all of my life." She met his gaze in the mirror. "It isn't a coincidence that God gave me that vision when I read the newspaper that morning and found Adela's ad. God isn't a God of coincidence. He is a God of purpose, not confusion." She resumed cutting, praying she was explaining herself without confusion.

"How do you know God won't change your mind?"

Why was he asking these questions? "The morning I drove into Mule Hollow I felt a special bond. Something reached out and touched me, and until I read that verse this morning, it hadn't fully registered that this was home. I felt a little like the prodigal son or something…not that I've been out eating with the pigs or anything, but you know what I mean."

"No. What do you mean? You are hardly the prodigal son."

Lacy nibbled her lower lip. Clint was pushing her. The question was why? Suddenly out of nowhere she knew it was time for her to bite the bullet. She didn't want to. But God was really thumping her on the head and she couldn't very well ignore Him.

"Clint, I'm fixing to be your friend and stick my nose where maybe it shouldn't be—" She paused when he raised an eyebrow. "Have you forgiven your mother for leaving you when you were a boy?"

Clint's eyes dulled. "Forgive her? Lacy, I know I'm supposed to. I know God forgave me, so as a Christian I'm supposed to forgive her. But honestly, until a few days ago it never crossed my mind that I should forgive my mother for what she did."

Lacy removed the cutting cape from his neck while praying for the words she needed. Heavy in thought, she leaned against the counter and toyed with the telephone cord.

"Forgiveness is weird in many ways," she said quietly. "It took me a while to forgive my dad. But after I forgave him it was I who received the reward. I mean my dad couldn't get the reward—I've never seen him again and I heard a rumor that he died. But I have a peace inside me now that wasn't there before I decided to forgive him and let it go."

"But the other night out in the storm—you were upset about your dad stealing your mother's dreams."

"I still have scars left over from his leaving my mom. And I'm human. Sometimes when I'm really down I'll sulk, and his leaving did change me and form me into the person that I am. I can't forget that. But I forgave him. And inside I know it. But most important, God knows it even when I'm having a pity party."

Clint studied her for a long moment and then he stood and headed toward his hat. "I can't say that I'm made of the same character as you. This just proves once more that you're a special lady, Lacy Brown. A special lady indeed."

With that he laid a twenty on the counter, touched her nose with the tip of his finger, then strode out the door of Heavenly Inspirations.

A lot of inspiring she had done. The man had issues and she hadn't helped him one bit.

Chapter Thirteen

The black night sky was wide-open, dotted with the sprinkle of stars and a mere thumbnail of a moon. Clint sat in a chair on his back patio staring into the dark heavens.

He didn't believe her. She had good intentions, but she didn't know what this town could do to a woman. She was too talented anyway. There were limitations to her talent here that she wouldn't have in a city. Financially speaking, she could make five times the salary elsewhere. She would see that soon.

He wasn't blaming her or looking down on her choices—it would just happen. He just prayed she left before he was in any deeper than he already was. Every time she spoke, he grew more intrigued by her heart. He had never been around anyone who earnestly sought out God's will like Lacy did.

He was a Christian, but he had to admit that sometimes he felt like he was simply going through the motions. Weeks would go by, and he would realize that he hadn't picked up his Bible except to carry it to church on Sunday morning.

That wasn't so with Lacy. As wacky as she could be, he knew that she walked closely with God. The Bible held the answers, but he knew that many times he didn't pick it up because he just didn't want to. There were days when he'd go all day thinking about needing to read the Bible, and then he would intentionally pick up a ranching magazine or turn on the television. It wasn't something he fully understood.

But he knew it was a rebellious action that stemmed from long ago.

Clint studied the stars. His mother used to study them with him. He saw her laying a blanket on the ground as she'd done when he was young. Then the three of them would lay on their backs, heads touching, and study the stars together. He remembered how once she'd told him that while they were looking up at heaven, God was looking down at them. She said He was smiling because they were looking in the right direction. It was a good memory, and for a moment he toyed with the idea of going to his office and opening the letter he'd received from her.

Lacy would have read the letter the moment it arrived in her mailbox. She had a heart that could expand

and embrace…. Closing his eyes, he rubbed the bridge of his nose. Lacy could embrace forgiving her father. But he wasn't as good a person as Lacy. Clint hardened his heart to the good memories of his mother. Though they pounded against its doors, they didn't last long.

His mother left him, cast him off without a backward glance. And she'd done it the very summer after they'd lain on the blanket and studied the stars.

Funny the difference a year could make.

Clint's heart was aching as he leaned forward in his chair, with his elbows on his knees, and studied the ground. It was rich and fertile for man and cattle, but not for a woman. Lacy didn't understand yet what remote, small-town life could do to a woman. And he couldn't forget.

And his heart couldn't watch someone else he loved walk away again.

And the letter… It could rot in his desk.

"Okay, move those hay bales over there," Lacy directed the two cowboys, Andrew and Bob. They were two great guys who were a part of the many who had been helping all day in the setup for tomorrow. Andrew was a dark-haired man with a funny bone and Bob was a tall, quiet loner who seemed content to help at whatever she asked. He didn't say much, but his presence was that of a giant. The two guys were great friends and Lacy could see why. They complemented each other like missing pieces to a puzzle. She couldn't wait until the right women came along that would fill their hearts just as perfectly. And they were ready, too.

Bob paused beside her now, balancing a square bale on his broad shoulder as if it were a mere brick. "Miss Adela asked me if I'd be in a special booth tomorrow."

"Oh, did she now?" Lacy smiled, leave it to Adela to know exactly the right guys for her *special* booth. The girls would be lining up for miles to buy lemonade from Bashful Bob. "And what did she tell you about her booth?"

He shifted and a faint tinge of pink crept into his cheeks. "It's a lemonade stand to help raise more advertisement money. I told her I didn't know anything about squeezing lemons, but she assured me the ladies wouldn't mind. Said she thought I was the man for the job, 'cause the ladies would want to watch me learn." His smile beamed and his dimples dug in deep. "I might be shy, but I'm no fool."

Lacy let out a hoot.

"Why, Bob Denton, you sneaky flirt. And I was calling you Bashful Bob."

Andrew sauntered over with a matching hay bale. "Lacy, don't let that shy exterior fool you. Bob is a lady magnet. Why do you think I'm his friend? The only problem is finding the ladies. You're our hero, or I guess I should say our heroine. If you can do for our love lives anything even close to the amazing stuff you've worked on this town, we just might not be lonesome cowboys anymore." He spun around on his boot heels with his empty arm flung wide. "Look at this place."

Watching him, Lacy felt a tug at her heart. These two sweet guys were typical of the men Mule Hollow had to offer: hardworking, good-natured men who would make wonderful husbands and fantastic dads. This plan for Mule Hollow had to work. It just had to.

Bob tipped his hat. "I guess we better get a move on putting this hay where it needs to be. See you later, Lacy."

She watched them stride away, hauling their heavy loads to their designated spots in front of the apple-green building and the periwinkle-blue one beside it. She plopped her hands on her hips and surveyed Main Street. It was looking pretty good. They had the cakewalk set up in front of Sam's so that the cakes could have a cool place to rest while waiting to be given away. The dunkin' booth, where a girl could step up and try and dunk a cowboy was next to the horseshoes, followed by rope tricks, then chip flinging at the end of the road. In the grassy area at the edge of town there was the three-legged race, the three-armed egg relay and a few other contests.

Tomorrow was the big day and time was running out. But everyone had their specific jobs and were busy with the last-minute details. They were all invested in this dream.

Sheri was heading up the talent committee. She and Sherri had discovered that there were quite a few singing cowboys out here on the range and they were putting them to good use at the afternoon picnic.

Norma Sue and Esther Mae were in charge of food preparation. Hank and Roy Don were legends around Mule Hollow for their chili and barbeque, so they were officially declared the cooks for the fair. Besides, it gave Sam the day off.

Adela was the official meet 'em and greet 'em host plus, she was overseeing the lemonade stand. She was also baking more cookies than Lacy had ever believed one woman could bake in a lifetime.

While everyone worked on their duties, Lacy was busy with hers as the official overseer of everything. She hadn't slept much since Tuesday, and though she had confidence that God was in control, sometimes she had to squelch that voice of worry. This was going to work and Mule Hollow was going to begin the path of reinvention tomorrow. Bob, Andrew and so many more were counting on it—

"Penny for your thoughts." Clint's familiar voice from just behind her jolted her from her brooding with a shiver of excitement.

"I'll take it," she said, spinning around to face the man who had been on her mind every moment she let her guard down. Her spirits lifted at his nearness.

"That cheap? Must be some pretty heavy thoughts

to sell out that low." His eyes glittered in the bright sunlight and his unshaven face gave him a dangerous persona. Upon closer inspection, he looked tired.

"My confidence is teetering," she admitted.

"*Your confidence.* I don't believe that for one minute. You are the gal who came blasting in here ready to take on anything." He surprised Lacy when he reached out and draped an arm about her shoulders and hugged her. "You've done a great job, Lacy. Chin up. No one but you could have done remotely what you have in just a few weeks. It's going to happen. I'm so proud of you."

Sighing, she gave in to the temptation to sink into his side and the support he was offering her. He was strong and solid. If she let herself, she knew it wouldn't be hard to stay in his arms forever. How much she'd missed him the past few days slammed into her. She had heard through Norma Sue that he'd been camping out all over his property trying to be in the right place at the right time to catch the rustlers who had struck again the evening she had cut his hair. She wished there was something she could do for him.

"Have you had any luck locating the cattle thieves?" she asked, pulling her feelings off her sleeve and focusing on something safer.

He released her and shook his head, watching as Andrew and Bob walked by with more hay bales on each shoulder. They tipped their hats, "Howdy, Clint. Glad you made it to the fun," Andrew said.

"Lacy sure knows how to give a party," added Bob.

Clint grinned. "Looks that way. You boys are doin' a fine job." He stuffed his hands into his pockets and shifted his weight to one leg before meeting her eyes.

"Haven't had a bit of luck with the cattle rustlers." He continued their conversation after the cowboys moved on. "The night we saw them was the last time I've been near them. I'm beginning to think I'm never going to see them again."

Lacy grinned and poked him in the chest playfully. "You just need me to find them for you. Next time I'm out on one of my midnight rides, I'll keep an eye out for them."

Clint's brow furrowed; his eyes hardened sternly. Not at all the reaction she was aiming for. Lacy squelched her smile. She didn't know what to make of the glint in his eyes.

She wasn't too sure she liked it.

When he spoke she *knew* she didn't like it. Not one bit!

"Lacy, I have some ideas about who might be involved in this, and I don't think it's a good idea for you to be driving that car of yours around late at night. You could get stranded again, and I might not be around to save you."

"Thank you very much, but I can take care of myself, Clint Matlock," she huffed.

"Lacy, I don't want to argue with you but you don't have any business out at night like that."

"Look, Clint." She faced him square and glared at him. And to think she had missed him! "You don't have any reason to be telling me what I can or should be doing." She bit her tongue to hold back on saying more. His demands disturbed her, though deep down she knew what he said had merit.

"Look, Lacy, all I'm saying is be careful. These cattle rustlers are professionals. They worry me, and I don't want you to be the one who comes up on them and catches them by surprise. I don't know what they might do. Brady has been doing some checking, and we have a good idea who they could be. If it is who we suspect, they have records and will not want to be caught again."

Lacy relaxed and forced her pride aside. "Sorry, I know what you're saying makes sense. I'm just so used to my drives that I can't stand not going when I feel like it."

Clint studied her for a long second. Then he reached out and touched a curl of her hair. "Tell you what, I haven't yet ridden in that thing you call a car. So the next time you go, come get me and take me for a spin."

Lacy didn't like the fact that she really liked his idea. But happiness welled within her and poured out in an ear-to-ear grin. "I just might do that, cowboy."

His lips did that slow slide into that crooked smile,

Lacy's heart did a giddyap right into her throat. Whoa, Nellie! This was getting ridiculous. And infatuating and dangerous and fun, she was thinking, when a little red sports car whizzed by and came to a halt at Adela's Boardinghouse.

"Wonder who that is?" Clint asked before she had a chance to voice the question.

Lacy started smiling again when a graceful woman, with long brown hair and legs to die for, stepped from the car. Every cowboy standing on Main Street had turned to watch as she straightened and glanced about the town.

Lacy sighed. "That, my friend, is Mule Hollow's future."

"Are you ready?"

Lacy licked her lips, grabbed hold of Clint's waist and nodded. "We can do this," she said, assessing the competition that stood along the starting line of the three-legged race.

Some of their competitors were J.P. and Sheri, Sheriff Brady and the elegant Ashby Templeton, who'd arrived the day before in the red sports car, a cute cowboy named Jake, Molly Popp, who'd also arrived the night before, and six other couples that included the three schoolteachers who were going to board at Adela's. Lacy felt pure joy at the picture they all made tied together, laughing and joking while they waited for Pete to fire the starting gun. This had so far been a glorious day.

There were people everywhere. Women had flocked to Mule Hollow from a radius of a hundred miles. Adela had been taking a poll and the reach of the ads, plus Molly's column had penetrated deep into the heart of Texas and even a few other states. This was proof that all things were possible with the Lord's help.

"On your mark." Pete's booming voice broke into Lacy's thoughts. She tightened her grip on Clint as he pulled her closer.

"Here we go," he said, his eyebrows knitted together in an ominous scowl. He meant business. Lacy giggled, looking up at him.

"Get set, go!"

In a roar of laughter, they were off. Guys were yelling and girls were laughing. Lacy concentrated on trying to keep her shorter stride with Clint's longer one, but they were really mismatched and clumsy. Beside them, Brady and Ashby were much more suited and started taking an early lead.

Clint glared over their way, "Oh, no, they don't," he growled, and nearly started dragging Lacy with him. Lacy started laughing so hard, she wasn't any help. Things went from bad to calamitous. In their haste, their rhythm got off. In the next instant, they were heading toward the ground in a pile of legs and arms.

Clint burst out laughing, too, as they tried to untangle themselves and stand again. They weren't alone on the ground. Half the lineup had taken the same detour and it now looked like a wrestling match rather than a three legged race.

Needless to say, Sheriff Brady and Ashby were victorious and showed no humility. They paraded their blue ribbon around proudly between the losers, goading that maybe everyone else could do better next year.

"What do you think, Lacy?" Clint asked after unraveling their legs and helping her up. "Is this going to happen again next year?"

"Are you kidding? We're going to practice every few weeks so we can make it more than ten feet next year."

Clint laughed and added dryly, "I meant the fair itself."

"Oh, yes, if I have any influence, this fair will become an annual event."

The event so far had been a raging success. Lacy hadn't seen so many happy cowboys in all of her life. The turnout had made believers of the majority of the guys. And the women were having such a great time that many of them had expressed a desire to look into property in the area. Mule Hollow had plenty of cheap real estate. It had been left behind by the families who had been forced to leave for lack of job opportunities.

The real-estate agent from Ranger had come down for the event and she was being bombarded with questions. If this frenzy continued, she'd said she might move to Mule Hollow.

Only time would tell how the town would really benefit from today, but Lacy was very optimistic.

"Are you interested in a glass of Adela's homemade lemonade?" Clint asked as they moved out of the way for the next heat of three-legged racers.

"Sure. But then I want to play Texas Frisbee."

"You really want to throw a cow chip?"

Lacy halted and plunked her hands to her hips. "Well, yeah. I bet I can fling one farther than you. You know," she said, jamming a thumb at herself in jest, "in high school I was district champ at the discus."

Clint shook his head. "You are a jack of all trades. A gymnast and discus star." He pushed his hat off his forehead with his thumb and scratched his temple. "What did you not do?"

Lacy started walking again. "A lot. Let's see, I wanted to play basketball but I was too small. I wanted to run hurdles but I was too small. I wanted to play volleyball but—"

Clint joined in. "You were too small."

"Uh-huh. So when I wanted to throw the discus the coach told me I was too skinny *and* too small. So my mom bought me a discus for my birthday and told me if I really wanted to do it, to do it and not let anyone tell me I couldn't. I practiced all summer and fall. When spring tryouts came, I told coach just to give me a chance to show him what I could do." Lacy slid a crooked eyebrow up and gave Clint a comical glare. "When I stepped up on that platform, everyone was laughing. And I mean laughing out loud, big-time. I didn't weigh eighty pounds wet. But I had worked on my form—you know the discus is really all about form—and mine was perfect. Anyway, I made the team and won district…but got creamed at the next level. I didn't care, I had proven to myself that hard work paid off."

They had reached the refreshment stand and stopped to wait in the lengthy line. Adela's plan had worked. Ladies waited patiently, dollars in hand, to see Andrew's smile and Bob's dimples up close while they passed out the lemonade.

"I bet you wish you'd never asked that question," she said, after they'd settled in for the wait.

Clint shook his head, "Actually I liked finding out what makes you tick."

"Oh, yeah." Lacy wrinkled her nose up and smiled. *Are you flirting with him, Lacy?*

"Oh, yeah," he said, reaching out and tugging at a strand of her hair. "I bet you gave your mama some gray hairs growing up."

"Yes, I can't deny the truth. I couldn't help myself. That was one of the reasons she put me in gymnastics early. She had to scrape the money together each month, but she said it gave my energy a positive release."

"What did you compete in? Wait, let me guess— those two bars that the girls fly from one to the other on."

"The uneven bars."

"That was it, wasn't it? I knew it had to be with the way you practically flew up into that tree the day Flossy was after your hide."

"You got it. I also did some other things, too." She didn't elaborate because they had reached the head of the line and Adela was beaming at them with a megawatt smile.

"Oh, Lacy, Clint, isn't this the most delightful day." Anticipating what they'd come for, she held out two glasses of lemonade. Each glass had sugar on the rim and a fat red cherry floating among the ice in the cool deep yellow drink.

"What a great drink, Adela! No wonder there has been a line here all day. And, yes, today is fantastic."

"Clint, how are you holding up with all these beautiful women running around?" Adela's direct question had Lacy choking on her lemonade.

Clint was just as surprised. He shifted his weight from one booted foot to the other, then planted his gaze on Lacy before answering.

"I'm holding up pretty good, considering I've had the prettiest gal of all tied to my leg half the day."

Lacy tried hard to keep from letting his good-natured banter plunge through her melting barriers.

But the butterflies nose-diving in her stomach were hard to ignore.

Adela handed them both a homemade cookie. "I'm glad to know you are an observant and smart man, Clint Matlock. You two enjoy the cookie and the rest of the day. You should go try out the three-handed egg race."

Lacy couldn't help laughing at the not-so-smooth attempt at matchmaking. "Thanks for the advice, Adela, but there are a couple of big fat cow chips across town with our names on them."

Clint tipped his hat at Adela as they started to leave. "This ought to be good, Adela. Maybe you should come over and watch. I think Lacy has the makings of a champion."

Lacy turned back to Clint and, linking her arm in his, pulled him away. "Come on with me, funny guy. I'm about to make a believer out of you. After all, I'm not just a pretty face."

"*That* is something I figured out a long time ago," he said, and pulled her into the laughing, swirling crowd.

Chapter Fourteen

"**Y**ou know what we should do," Lacy exclaimed, causing everyone sitting in Sam's to look her way. "We need to come up with a business big enough to employ a lot of women."

Everyone who had been involved in masterminding the fair day was settled into chairs at Sam's place. They were exhausted, tired and *more* exhausted. The day had been an unbelievable success. Adela's place was packed, and if there had been a fifty-room hotel, it would probably have been full. Now it was about midnight, and everyone had gathered at Sam's to discuss the day. They were far too keyed-up to sleep.

Lacy was nearly bouncing off the walls and was afraid she was making everyone nervous. But she knew her idea was good.

"Hey, Lacy girl, that might be a good idea," boomed Esther Mae.

"There's a town not too far from here," added Norma Sue. "It has a huge furniture store that takes up half the old town. They just knocked out walls and connected the buildings. I heard they ship that furniture all over the place."

"Lacy—" Sheri yawned "—you know that town not too far from Dallas that has those baskets…oh, and the one not too far from there that makes those fruitcakes. They ship those things all over the world."

"Yeah, that's what I'm talking about." She started pacing.

"What we need to do," Adela said, "is start thinking of everything that might be a profitable endeavor."

"The way I see it," Lacy said, her mind humming with ideas, "we had a great response from the women from surrounding towns, but they need income in order to move here. I hadn't even thought of that until today. There are more people than just the teachers who might consider moving here if there were jobs for them."

Clint raised his hand and an eyebrow while looking at Lacy for acknowledgment. She smiled broadly at his schoolboy impersonation and pointed at him. "Clint, you may have the floor."

"I was thinking maybe I could hire a truckload of them. I need somebody to patrol for rustlers that I don't seem able to track myself."

Everyone, including Clint, roared with laughter.

Lacy shook her head, enjoying his playful side, and at the same time feeling kind of sorry for him because she knew he really did need to catch the rustlers.

Adela stood and smoothed the front of her cotton paisley dress. It barely had any wrinkles, and one would never have guessed she'd worn it all day and night.

"I guess what we should do is call it a night, and pray that the Lord will lead us in this endeavor. He's done a wonderful job so far by sending us Lacy and Sheri first, and then giving us this great day."

Everyone stood in agreement and, after hugs and good-nights, agreed to pray diligently.

Lacy had enjoyed her day at the fair more than anything she'd done in her life. And that was because of Clint. They had spent the entire day together without ever really planning to. It had simply seemed right. For Lacy, the lines between why she had come to Mule Hollow and why she couldn't fall in love with Clint were blurring.

Fall in love with Clint—her thoughts were running away with themselves. She'd meant why she couldn't *date* Clint.

She was about to climb into her Caddy, when the subject of her confusion strode over, dropped his arm over her shoulders and gave her a friendly squeeze.

"I had a great time today."

"Me, too," she said, realizing how much she enjoyed the gesture.

"Sorry I doubted all of this early on; I believe from here on out I'm going to have a lot more faith." He released her and headed toward his truck.

Watching him walk away, Lacy's heart was pounding and her entire wonderful day was replaying before her eyes.

"See you at church in the morning," he called. Looking back at her, he paused while opening his truck door.

He was gorgeous. "Oh, yes. Bright and early." She watched him get in the truck then before she climbed into her Caddy she checked the time on her watch. It was one o'clock in the morning. Church started at ten o'clock. Which meant…

Only nine more hours until she could see Clint Matlock again.

"Okay, now you roll the dough like this." Lacy took her rolling pin, dusted it with a little flour and then began rolling out the thick ball of blackberry cobbler dough. Beside her, Clint stood watching as if this were the most important bit of instruction he would ever get. He was making her nervous. She'd been surprised when he'd told her he had something he wanted to bring by her house after church, if she were going to be there. After she had assured him that she would be, he'd come by bearing a bag of frozen blackberries, blackberries he'd obtained from Norma Sue's freezer since the season had ended at the beginning of the summer.

Lacy had been tickled by his presumption that she would drop everything and show him how to make *The Best Cobbler in the World.* Which she did, not that she had anything else to do. She was actually thrilled to be spending another Sunday afternoon with Clint, which she had decided could become habit forming.

And dangerous. Her kitchen was a small space with a low ceiling and the minute Clint had entered it he'd seemed to surround Lacy. Her senses were on overload.

"So now we have it rolled out." She paused and used the back of her wrist to scratch the top of her nose. "Now we get to cut it in strips."

Clint relaxed against the counter as he watched what she was doing beside him. His arms were crossed over his broad chest; his position had him facing Lacy. She reached for the knife she would use to cut the pastry and paused before cutting.

"You sure you know how to use that thing?" he asked playfully, leaning his shoulder into hers.

Lacy frowned and pointed the tip of the knife at him. "You would be surprised at what I can do, Buster."

"Actually, Lacy, there isn't anything you could do that would surprise me."

Feeling a touch of pride at his words, Lacy started slicing the dough.

"Although, finding out you could cook is a stretch of my imagination." He nodded toward the pastry and the hot berry mixture waiting for the pastry, to finish it off.

Lacy gave him a mock look of disgust. "And just why is that?"

"I don't know." He sobered. "You don't come across as the homemaker type."

Lacy's pride plummeted. Once before he had insinuated that she was like his mother, and now she wondered… "Clint," she ventured. Uncertain how to broach the subject she faltered as she placed the pastry into the bubbling berries. "Do I remind you of your mother?" Well, that was being subtle! Way to go, Lacy.

Beside her he stiffened, then reached out and touched her nose.

"You had a little…uh, flour, um there." Their eyes met and held.

Lacy refused to relinquish her question to his diversion tactic. "Do I?" Please say no.

He shrugged. "Some."

Some. Lacy wanted to cry. Her nose started to burn and her eyes started to sting but she refused to let her lip quiver. She stared at him and fought the insult down with every ounce of self-control that she possessed. Her eyes would not dampen. "I see," she said after she could. "I believe this is ready to go into the oven." She picked up the pan of cobbler and carried it to the oven. Clint followed her. Drat the man.

She had not come to Mule Hollow to fall in love. She had come to prove to the Lord that He was King of her life by giving His vision her total concentration for a while.

But she hadn't been able to do that. She felt like a failure, because before she could be a witness for Christ to even one person in her new salon, she had fallen in love.

And she had fallen in love with a guy whom she reminded of the lowest of the low. A woman who would desert her child.

It was all too much for even Lacy to comprehend. The room had become very quiet. She closed the oven door, then leaned her head against the cabinet. *Dear Lord, help me.*

Clint touched her shoulder. "Lacy." He was standing behind her and his voice was gentle.

No! "Clint, I don't feel so good. I think you should go."

"Lace—"

"Really, Clint." She turned to face him, then brushed past him before he could stop her. "I'm tired from yesterday and last night and I want to lie down."

"Lacy, I—"

She cut him off. Spinning around, she glared at him. "Clint, I want to lie down and *you* need to leave. *Now.*"

She didn't want to hear any more. She had been a fool anyway falling in love with the first guy who came along. How fickle was that!

To make things worse, finding out the type of person she came across as proved her greatest fears. It was as if the cock had crowed three times. Her uncontrolled personality, her mouth, caused the world to see a bum package. Her fickle heart caused Lacy to see the same.

"Maybe you're right," Clint said, backing to the door. "Get some rest. I need to get back to work anyway." He tipped his hat, spun on his heel and walked out the door.

Belligerently, Lacy glared after him. She would not cry. She would get back to doing what she came to Mule Hollow for in the first place. She would ask God for forgiveness and she would resume her original plan.

And she would ignore the ripping, wrenching agony exploding in her heart.

His mother wanted his forgiveness.

Clint sat at his desk, the letter, neatly typed and to the point, lay open before him…an answered prayer gone bad. After days of struggling with how he'd hurt

Lacy's feelings, he'd finally set his backbone straight and faced the facts. He needed to open the letter and try and face the past that threatened any future he might have with Lacy.

So he'd opened the letter.

And for the life of him, he didn't know what to do now. He was a man used to making hard, quick decisions. He made them all day long. And now he felt like a lost little kid.

But he wasn't a boy anymore. He was a full-grown man who needed to act like one.

But forgiveness… He stared out the window, across the open range his mother had left behind so easily. She'd walked away from him just as casually as she'd left the land. And she'd never looked back. Until now.

Clint rubbed his temple; the dull throb of a headache was setting in. He was a man. A churchgoing Christian man, A man who took pride in the fact that he'd overcome years of hurt and endless nights of boyhood tears, because God, ever the comforter, had wrapped him in His sheltering arms when he'd hurt the worst.

But forgive her.

Clint pushed away from his desk and stood. The knot in the pit of his stomach wasn't from hunger, and the stinging around his eyes wasn't from allergies. He was a man, all right, a man who hadn't needed God's comfort in a very long time.

Picking up his hat, he strode from the room and headed for the barn and a hard ride on a horse that didn't want to be broken any more than Clint wanted to think about forgiving the woman he'd spent the better part of his life trying to forget.

He knew it would take more than a few nice words to break that colt, and one lousy letter wasn't doing anything for Clint except opening old wounds.

"So what do you think about giving me some highlights?" Molly Popp asked Lacy.

It was Tuesday and they were looking at each other in the mirror. Molly had stayed on for a week while she finished her column about the town and the fair day. Lacy had been pleased when she'd walked in this morning. Clients would be sparse for the first few months, and for a person like herself, sitting was not a virtue she took to with alacrity.

"Highlights would look great on your chestnut hair." She hoped she didn't sound too anxious.

"Then go to it."

Lacy grabbed a tray with all of her foils and went about setting everything up for the color process. She and Molly chatted rapidly about the fair and the ongoing plans to encourage women to establish themselves in Mule Hollow. Lacy was pleased that Molly had such a positive outlook on the idea. She had informed Adela that morning that she would be going back to Houston, closing out her small apartment there, and at the end of the month she would be back. She would then become the third new citizen of Mule Hollow since the newspaper ad had been placed, Lacy and Sheri being first and second.

Molly was a beauty. She had a mane of hair the color of burnt umber that flowed in waves of lively movement every time she talked or turned her head. She was very easy to talk to, which was probably a good thing since she was a reporter. Her eyes were an alert, vivid green. Her hands moved as she spoke and she had a habit of inclining her head to the right when she listened to what you were saying. She was a beautiful, warm and intelligent woman and she didn't know the Lord at all.

"So you came all the way out here because *God* told you to."

Molly's inflection was proof enough that she couldn't know God, or she would have known that what Lacy had done wasn't all that unusual. People listened to God's voice every day. Because she followed His direction, a few hundred miles wasn't a big deal. She hadn't had to sacrifice anything. She was no martyr and certainly no saint. Of course, depending on who you asked, she might be considered crazy. And from the look on Molly's face, this is what Molly thought of Lacy.

"What's the difference in my following Christ out here and you following your heart?"

"Well, hold on. Let me think this out." Molly was different than Lacy in that she tended to think before she spoke. Lacy wondered if she hung out with Molly long enough, some of that habit would rub off on her.

"I guess the big difference is I came here first before committing to it. You on the other hand had already committed yourself, sight unseen. How could you do that?"

"Easy. It's called faith. I trust my heavenly Father and am willing to go where He leads me. Now, because I did this doesn't mean that I'm a saint or anything. I'm still plugging along, botching things up as I go. But I'm hoping and praying that I'm getting something right as I go."

She had really been wondering about that for the past four days. With Clint, she hadn't gotten anything right. Not so much in what she said but by her actions. And obviously she'd bungled that up hopelessly with her mouth and her heart.

Oh, how she'd missed him. How easily and subtly her heart had betrayed her. After she had thrown him out of her house—his house actually—she realized that she'd admitted that she had fallen in love with him. Her love had clicked into place like a natural fact. It was as if the love had been there since the beginning of time, waiting for Clint and Lacy to walk into it. Or at least Lacy…. Clint was the one who thought she reminded him of his good-for-nothing mother. *Forgive me, Lord. I know I'm not supposed to judge, but I do judge her and I can't seem to stop.*

She had to forget about Clint and place herself in the present, walking Molly through her questions about faith. And while she was at it, she might need to work on putting her own faith back into action.

Chapter Fifteen

Clint slammed the door to his pickup and yanked his hat from his head. Every cowboy who worked for him was gathered in the stable yard, and he knew by their expressions that they were wary of his fury.

"Four nights and thirty more head gone." At the rate they were going, he might as well get out of the cattle business of his own accord. He'd rather do that than be stolen blind by the bunch of parasites who'd chosen him as their host.

"Tonight I want them stopped. They're coming in at the outer sections of land, and that's where I want you. I want every inch of the outskirts of the ranch under surveillance. Forget about the interior—it's the far sections they keep ripping off."

"But what if they decide to come closer in tonight?" Merle Jansen asked. He was a skinny twenty-something with a gambling habit and a lazy streak that worked on Clint's nerves. But tonight he had just asked the key question Clint had been waiting for. He'd finally figured out that someone was working from the inside, and his hunch had been that it was Merle. His question made Clint all the more positive that his hunch was right.

Clint leveled his gaze at Merle. "They haven't come in yet, and I don't see why they'd start tonight. Therefore," Clint paused and swept his gaze across the group, including everyone, not wanting to cause Merle to think he suspected anything, "I don't want any manpower wasted within the inner limits. You each know your stakeout positions. Be there. I'm not losing another heifer to these bozos."

With that Clint stalked into the office and slammed the door. His plan was set. He was about to be rid of the thorn in his side, and all he had to do was wait and watch. Brady had been in contact with the Texas district field inspector and they were on the lookout for his cattle at auctions across Texas and New Mexico. Now all he had to do was catch Merle's cohorts, and if his hunch was right, they were going to come right to him tonight.

Clint's mind was full, he needed closure on the rustlers so he could think straight about all the personal issues bearing down on him. Inside information was the only way the rustlers were getting away with their stealing, time after time. It had been an accident that he'd seen them in action the night of the rainstorm. He'd realized finally that he wasn't supposed to be where he was that night. He'd come in from his stake-out early, and Lacy hadn't been in the equation at all. She'd been an accident waiting to happen, with all of her midnight excursions, and the rustlers hadn't figured on her random outings.

Lacy's midnight drives worried him. It was only a matter of time before she ran into the rustlers again. His fear for her was all the more reason for him to want to finish them off tonight.

Tramping into the house, he hung his hat on the rack, removed his boots and his socks, padded into the kitchen. It had been a hard week. And he wasn't talking about rustlers. He was thinking about Lacy.

Rolling his long sleeves up to his elbows, he turned on the water at the sink, and washed his hands, lost in thought as he scrubbed. Leaving the sink to yank open the icebox door for something to eat, all he could see was the look on Lacy's face as she'd told him to leave her home.

Other than the letter from his mother, Lacy was all he'd thought about since she'd stopped talking to him Sunday afternoon. He'd dealt with the issue of the rustlers because he had to, but Lacy, sweet Lacy, had been on his mind as he'd wrestled with his plans for their capture.

He hadn't meant to make her mad, to hurt her feelings. But as he was standing there watching her facial expression crumble, all of his feelings and fears rushed into combat in his heart. When he'd let her throw him out, he'd known exactly what he was doing and what he'd become. A coward.

She *was* like his mother. He'd known that from the first moment he'd met her. But she was all the good that his mother possessed, not the bad. And yet he'd still left, letting her believe he thought the worst of her. Because deep inside he was afraid no matter how much she loved the Lord, no matter how much she might love him, if he were lucky…one day she still might leave.

Watching those beautiful Pacific Ocean eyes of hers battle back a tidal wave of hurt, he'd realized how much more it would pain him to see her go.

God help me, but I couldn't take it.

Ramming his hands through his hair, he left them there as he leaned his elbow against the refrigerator and let the war inside of him rage. What was he going to do? She couldn't be changed. He wouldn't want her to. It was that fly-by-the-seat-of-her-pants kind of fun spirit that drew him to her. But it was the same spirit that scared him away.

Dear Lord, he prayed, standing there with the icy air surrounding him. *I don't know what to do. I need Your guidance. I need to let the hurt from my mother go, but I can't find the forgiveness inside of me. I know that I can't let the pain of yesterday continue to rule me today. And I know if I can't forgive my mother, I can't heal and move forward. I need Your help. I can't do this on my own. I'm praying this as Lacy would pray, not my will but Your will, amen.*

Clint stepped back from the freezer door and allowed it to close. He felt drained and had lost his appetite. His prayer hadn't lifted him up. If anything, it left him feeling even more restless.

Empty.

But he knew where to find his answers.

Turning toward the counter, he stared at the Bible lying there. Waiting.

It had been a long time since he'd picked his Bible up out of want instead of habit. It usually lay on that counter everyday except Sunday mornings when he picked it up on his way out the door to church. Now picking it up, he walked into the den, turned on the lamp beside his chair and sat down.

And then he opened his Bible.

The wind whipped at Lacy's face and hair as she sped down the deserted road. Easing up on the gas pedal, she checked the time on the dash—2:00 a.m. She'd been smokin' the roads for an hour, and still, sleep remained out of reach.

Her life had seemed so focused only a few weeks ago…and now she was lost as to what she should do.

Even the driving experience, the wind in her face and the starry night couldn't cheer her.

Depressed and getting pretty pitiful wallowing in misery, Lacy braked the Caddy to a jolting halt in the center of the road. "Why, Lord? Why did You let me fall in love with Clint Matlock?"

She had spent the week working in her salon in Mule Hollow. The place she had come to, to prove her love for God. The town she'd come to love. The town she'd felt she belonged from that first whisper of hope she'd sensed when she'd closed her eyes that first morning. She'd come to change, to prove to herself that she wasn't a fly-by-night fence rider. And she'd failed. In every way.

A sound in the night broke through Lacy's distress and she lifted her head from where she'd leaned her brow on the steering wheel. As she scanned the darkness, a chill raced up her spine. Given the screams of crickets and the burps of bullfrogs, Lacy wasn't exactly certain there was anything else she could have heard. As she focused on her surroundings and drew away from her weeping heart, she became aware of how alone she was in the remote back roads.

She really wasn't that far from home; as a matter of fact, Clint's home also wasn't too far away. But she was alone, it was after two in the morning and there was definitely something making noise out there in the dark.

There…a flicker of light. The faint murmur of an engine as the light bobbed then angled slightly away and went out.

Rustlers! The rustlers were back.

Lacy turned off her lights hoping they hadn't spotted them yet, and then she guided her Caddy to the side of the road and turned off the ignition.

It was the same as the night she and Clint had encountered each other and the rustlers. The distance might not be as far though, and there was no mud. But she felt sure that just as they'd disappeared quickly that first night, they'd do the same tonight. They'd get away. They would be ghosts once more and it might be weeks before anyone saw them again. Clint would lose more livestock. Her adrenaline started pumping.

She climbed out of the car. "Not tonight, buckos," she whispered to the darkness. She'd learned after the storm to dress for her late-night drives. She wore a soft cotton shirt, blue jeans, boots and socks. She was prepared for anything.

Her adrenaline was surging as she stared into the distance, through a stand of trees looming like a black wall in the darkness. She knew they were out there.

Clint's thieves. Mule Hollow would never be clear to flourish if these rustlers weren't stopped. Why, what single woman would want to settle in the country knowing the hills were alive with hoodlums. Already Molly had found out about the rustlers and was preparing for an article, but the only story Mule Hollow needed about rustlers was about their capture.

Her decision made, Lacy stepped toward the fence. "Dear Lord, help me," she whispered. "I'm about to get into trouble."

She had made it through the pasture, which hadn't been an easy task in the dark. Especially when she started thinking about snakes, rattlesnakes to be exact. She prayed harder than she'd prayed in a long time, for protection from her stupidity. But she had forged on, knowing that Clint's rustlers needed catching.

In the darkness she could hear the bawling of cattle and the soft curses of men. The air was heavy with the scent of pine. As she drew closer to the faint voices, she found a small cluster of pine trees and a gully she hadn't counted on. Half rolling, half walking and crawling, she managed to make the steep embankment in one piece. At the bottom she had to cross a small stream that was barely to her ankles and then climb back up the other side. It was a hard treacherous climb in the dark.

When she finally crawled over the edge she lay sprawled on her back looking up at the heavens. She was breathing hard from the exertion of climbing up the ravine. The sounds of the cattle were much closer now and she had to ignore the first tremors of fear. They rolled over her in a wave.

There was no room for fear out here. This was for Clint. This was for Mule Hollow.

Even if Clint thought so little of her, she knew she had to do whatever she could to help him. She loved him.

That thought was what had kept her from turning back when visions of rattlesnakes threatened to overtake her courage.

She loved him, and even if there might never be a miracle and he could love her, she could do this for him and the town. *Give me strength, Lord.*

Knowing it was time to move again, Lacy sat up, rolled onto her knees then crawled to the trees. She could see lights now. Not big lights but flashlights. They bobbed at the back of a huge trailer into which two men were loading the last of the cattle.

She had made it just in time. They looked as if they were nearly finished, and she knew they would be driving off into the night. This would be the last anyone saw of them for who knew how long.

Her thoughts were rioting with her next move—when suddenly a hand slid over her mouth. Her heart stopped and before she could react, she was yanked hard against a rock-solid frame.

"Don't make a sound," her captor bit out in a gravelly hiss against her ear. "Don't even move."

What was this woman up to now? Clint held Lacy against his chest and waited for her to stop squirming.

She was stronger than she looked and he had to hang on to her mouth harder than he wanted to in order to stop her from crying out.

"Lacy, it's me," he managed to grit out before she bit him. "Clint. Hold still, or they're going to know we're out here."

Lacy stilled in his arms and turned her head to look into his face. She couldn't see him in the shadows of the trees, but she nodded. He removed his hand. Immediately she spun around to face him. He had to bend down a bit to make out her angry whisper.

"You scared the daylights out of me. What are you doing here?"

"I want to know what *you're* doing here."

He was watching the movements of the men who were not more than ten yards away from them. They hadn't heard them yet but Lacy's zealous nature was not on their side.

"I'm trying to catch your rustlers." As if suddenly remembering them, she turned quickly away from him. He moved in close behind her, wishing with all of his soul that she hadn't shown up here. Not when he could smell victory over the cattle thieves.

What would he do now? His plan hadn't included endangering Lacy.

The men loaded the last steer into the trailer and closed it up. Then without a word they went up front to the truck and climbed in.

Clint knew he was about to miss his chance. His hunch about his hired hand, Merle, being in on the rustling from the inside had been right. Clint had staked out here in the hope that they'd come after this particular herd because many of them were pregnant and ready to drop calves any day. What better way to multiply your money than to steal two for one?

"We can't let them go!" Lacy exclaimed as the truck engine purred to life and the trailer's taillights blinked. She made a move as if to follow and Clint grabbed her.

"Whoa, Lacy. You're not going anywhere."

She twisted around, and he knew she was glaring daggers at him, even if he couldn't see her eyes.

"We can't let them go."

Clint mirrored her exasperation. He'd planned to sneak a ride on the trailer as it was pulling away, find out where they were taking the cattle, then report his findings to Brady. But he couldn't risk that with Lacy along. Jumping on trailers and risking his own hide was one thing, putting Lacy in jeopardy wasn't an option he was willing to take. Dropping his hand from her arm, he snatched his hat from his head and raked a hand through his hair, thinking out a new plan of attack.

Unfortunately that was the opening Lacy needed. She shot out of the protection of the trees and after the retreating shape of the cattle trailer.

* * *

Sprinting to the trailer, which was picking up speed, Lacy flung herself onto the bumper before she really had a chance to realize what she was doing.

Her impetuousness had taken over once more and she was just going to have to deal with it.

Cows were bellowing, shuffling about, adjusting to the movement of the rough ride. Lacy clung for dear life to the hard steel bars and for a split second she thought about dropping off. Then she found herself staring through the trailer bars at the huge dark eyes of a young heifer crammed inside the trailer. Its face was illuminated slightly by the red glow of the tail-lights, and as Lacy hung there it jabbed her cheek with its wet, slimy nose, as if asking for help.

"Okay, girl," Lacy groaned, hanging on tighter. "I'm going to get you out of there.

"Lacy Brown, are you crazy?" Clint snapped, swinging onto the trailer beside her, not happy he'd been forced to chase after her. "You're going to get yourself killed." This was not his plan.

"I am not. These guys are cattle thieves. They're not killers."

"You don't know that. Now, drop off while you still can," he demanded. "Lacy, I won't have you in harm's way. Drop off *now*."

"No." She scrambled over the back of the trailer gate and balanced herself inside between the gate and the side railing. Looking down at the dark shapes of the bumping, shuffling animals she felt a bit of fear, at least she saw no horns in this section of the trailer.

That was a good thing.

Clint dropped in beside her, muttering something she couldn't understand, but in the darkness his anger was almost visible.

Well, he could just be angry. She'd started this dance and she planned to finish it. Clutching the rails like a monkey over an alligator pit, Lacy tried to ignore him, but when the truck came to an abrupt halt, she lost her grip and slipped.

Clint shot a hand out and grasped her around the waist and smoothly swung her up against his chest. Obviously he'd had much more skill in the back of a trailer than she had.

After the trailer started moving again, it hit a bump and Clint wrapped his arm tighter around Lacy. He gripped the rail for support with his free hand and fought to keep the shuffling cattle off of her with his body. One wrong move and they could easily be crushed by the huge beasts.

"Don't you know when to control your impulses?" he asked, annoyed that she was here, but glad she hadn't come upon the rustlers alone. He thanked God that He'd put him in her path tonight.

She twisted around to face him in the tight corner where he had her secured. Despite everything, he wanted to kiss her right there. It didn't make any sense; the woman drove him crazy with her spontaneity. She was uncontrollable.

But he loved her.

He had admitted this to himself that afternoon while he read his Bible.

He had no claim on her. She'd made that clear over and over. And after this little stunt, he was beginning to question his sanity in wanting to call her his…"forgetting those things which are behind, and reaching forth unto those things which are before."

The words in Philippians 3:13 echoed through his heart. God had led him to that verse as he'd read His word. Clint knew it hadn't been a coincidence that this was the scripture God had sent to him. His mother's rejection was behind him and Lacy's love, if he could hope, was before him. God was letting him know that he needed to move forward.

The terrifying question plaguing Clint was how could he live never knowing what she would do next? A little crazy driving, a cute, hot temper, mixed with a soft heart and a bewildering amount of determination to achieve her goals—these things, surprisingly enough, drew him to her. But this reckless willingness to endanger herself…he wasn't sure he could handle.

Even with God's assurances.

Chapter Sixteen

Lacy stared between the cattle trailer's iron bars into the dark night speeding past. Clint's nearness was making her senses wobble more than the trailer ride. She had to keep reminding herself how little he thought of her and that she had goals to achieve that had nothing to do with loving him.

She stole a thoughtful glance at Clint. He was on his cell phone talking to Sheriff Brady. Clint had been trying for the past fifteen minutes to get a call through to him, which was no easy task in these parts. Now that he'd connected, he was giving Brady as much information on their steadily moving location as he could, just in case they couldn't get a connection again. Staring back into the darkness she fought to ignore his presence beside her.

Life had its little jokes.

Could she change Clint's opinion of her? Could she prove she was worthy of his love, that she wouldn't abandon him or their children if she were so lucky? It was something she'd pursue if she hadn't gotten them into a situation they couldn't get out of…

"Brady's on his way," Clint said, breaking into her thoughts. "Or at least on his way to this area. He's going to call Ranger's sheriff department for backup."

"Do you know where we are?" Lacy asked, hoping.

"Not exactly. It's hard to know in the dark, the last road mark I was able to give them was before we got on this dirt road. Hopefully this is the only gravel road off of a farm-to-market road near a power tower."

Lacy tried not to worry. But she knew that she had gotten them into this by her impulsive lack of thinking.

After what seemed like forever, the trailer slowed. Clint placed a protective hand on her shoulder as the cattle shifted and bumped them around. The trailer passed over a cattle guard and Clint leaned close.

"We need to be ready to hop off this thing before they get to the corral," he said near her ear.

Nodding, Lacy ignored the tingling sensation his breath sent skittering over her skin, and she started climbing out of the trailer.

"Be careful," he said, holding her arm for support as she shimmied over the rail.

Lacy concentrated on keeping her footing. Once she had her feet securely planted on the bumper, she scooted out of Clint's way. "Your turn," she said, then watched him climb easily out beside her.

The trailer bounced over a rough spot but he maneuvered out onto the bumper with ease.

Holding her gaze, he suddenly leaned in and kissed her. "You are a beautiful woman, Lacy Brown. A handful of trouble, but beautiful."

There he went, confusing her again!

"Come on," he whispered, as if nothing had just passed between them. "Let's get into the shadows of that barn."

Feeling off balance, she waved a hand at him. "Lead the way."

He grabbed her hand and they hopped from the trailer together. Fading into the night, they circled out of the way of the headlights.

"Where do you think we are?" she asked, once they were safely flattened against the wall of the barn. This was no time to figure out what was going on between them. That would have to wait, even though her heart was racing and it had nothing to do with rustlers.

Echoing moos and the heavy thud of hooves signaled the cattle were being unloaded. Clint snuck a peek and didn't answer her. Lacy bent around him and snatched a look of her own. In the beam of a spotlight, two cowboys moved the cattle into an empty roping pen.

"Do you recognize either of them?" she asked softly.

"Get back, Lacy. I don't want you getting hurt," he said without answering her question.

Lacy straightened. "I'm not going to get hurt. Clint Matlock, you're the most maddening man."

"Not now, Lacy," he sighed, grasping her arms and holding her still. Leaning forward he rested his forehead against hers.

The rising protest congealed in her throat. Seconds passed and she could only stand there, wondering at the thoughts passing through his mind.

At last, keeping his forehead against hers he said, "My plan was to find this place and wait for backup, it wasn't to get caught standing here having this conversation. This isn't your fight and I don't want you taking any more chances. I want you to stay here while I get a closer look. Is that too much to ask?"

"It *is* my fight," she whispered, glancing about, fearing Clint was right and they would be discovered because of her runaway mouth. "These men are threatening the good reputation of Mule Hollow. As a business owner and a citizen, that makes everything they do my concern." She squared her shoulders. "I've already told you not to worry about me. I'm not *your* concern. Besides, I can take care of myself. And after all, I got us into this. Remember."

Briskly he slid his hands up and down her arms, as

if fighting his own conflicting emotions, then he pulled her gently against him.

A shaking, she could have handled. A hug, caught her off guard, more so than the earlier kiss had and her heart swelled.

Breaking away, she stomped toward the far end of the barn away from the light. Away from Clint and the things he made churn inside her. One minute he was comparing her to his *mother* and the next he was kissing her, hugging her, playing with her heart. No! Do not allow this.

"Where are you going?"

"I'm going to find out where we are, and figure a way to catch these guys." As she spoke, she concentrated on not falling over an old tire.

"I don't want them knowing we're here, Lace—"

His voice sounded funny all of a sudden and Lacy looked up to see why he'd quit griping.

The shotgun stopped her dead in her tracks.

"Too late," said a voice from the darkness. "Looks like I already know you're here."

This is not good. Lacy stared at the barrel of the gun as the man behind the voice stepped from the end of the barn. He was tall, shrouded in black, with a cigarette hanging from the corner of his mouth. The red tip bounced with each word he spoke.

"Stay calm, Lacy," Clint urged, touching the small of her back with his hand.

Too late, Lacy's adrenaline was up, plopping her hands on her hips, she glared at the cigarette-smoking bandit. "*He* better stay calm."

Clint jabbed her.

"Me?" Cigarette-butt chuckled wickedly. "I think you've got this little situation confused. I'm the one with the gun. Now move it."

The cold metal against her shoulder brought a little sanity to Lacy's insane behavior. He pushed her shoulder with the double-barreled shotgun and she decided maybe now was the time to do as he instructed.

"Don't hurt the lady," Clint said, a menacing edge to his voice that exceeded their captor's.

"I'll do what I want. And now I want you to move. If you don't, I'll shoot her."

"Do as he says, Lacy." Clint turned and Lacy followed him toward the sound of the cattle being unloaded.

Lacy decided she didn't like the gun jabbing her in the back at all. "You'll never get away with this," she snapped.

"Lacy, be quiet."

Even though fear was screaming inside of her, Lacy ignored it. "I will not be silent, Clint Matlock!"

"So that's who you are," said gun-toting Cigarette-butt. "Get tired of us ripping you off?"

"You're right about that, bucko," Lacy answered for Clint. "He's tired of you jerks."

"Lacy, for crying out loud—" Clint muttered in exasperation. "Would you cut it out? I'm trying to save you here. Or hadn't you noticed the man has a gun pointed at you?"

They'd reached the front of the barn and stepped into the view of the other rustlers.

"Looky what I found draggin' around the back of the barn," Cigarette-butt called to his friends. Turning, they stared into the spotlight hanging on the barn behind Lacy and Clint, then sauntered over.

Lacy cringed. They looked like the big, the bad and definitely the *ugly*. Up close she could see that one even had a patch over his eye.

"Well, look what we have here," One-eye said, leering at them.

"Knock it off, Austin," Clint drawled.

Lacy shot a glare at Clint. "How'd you know his name?"

"The patch. Brady gave me some descriptions he'd come up with from the Cattle Raisers Association field inspectors. There aren't too many rustlers with one eye. It seems Austin and his boys pull these scams off all over the country. The One-eyed Rustler is wanted in five states. We had a hunch it was them. The patterns matched their previous jobs."

"Why didn't you tell me?" Lacy asked, stung by the fact that he hadn't confided in her.

"Because it was my problem."

She stared at him to no effect. He hadn't taken his eyes off of the one-eyed Austin. "You could have told me." She knew she was being childish…. They were standing in the middle of a bunch of could-be cutthroats and she was hurt because Clint hadn't told her he knew who the thieves were.

"Yeah, Clint, you could have told her," Austin mimicked, stepping up close to Lacy. When she moved to back away, he wrapped an arm around her waist and yanked her against him. "This could be a fun night."

In his arms, Lacy felt the first real fear that she had ever felt. Austin leaned his head in close to her; she twisted, averting her face from his hot breath. Her gaze met Clint's and her heart stopped. His expression had turned murderous, his eyes, hard as stone.

When Austin ran a hand holding a pistol along her jaw, Clint lunged. "Keep your hands off her—" He never saw the butt of the shotgun as it slammed into his shoulder, barely missing his skull.

Lacy screamed as she watched Clint go down on one knee, saw the sick grin that played across Cigarette-butt's face. She tried to bend down next to Clint but Austin held her firmly away. "Clint," she cried as Austin placed the barrel of his pistol against Clint's temple. She went very still.

Dear, Lord, please don't let anything happen to Clint. And deliver us from this mess I've gotten us into. She prayed like she'd never prayed before.

"Lacy," Clint said, breaking into her prayer with a voice as hard as concrete. "Do exactly as they tell you. Austin, as far as I know, you don't have killing on your record. I wouldn't start now."

Austin pressed the barrel more snugly against Clint's skull. "I've never been in this situation before. If I had, I might have made my first kill a long time ago."

His chuckle sent shivers down Lacy's spine.

"We have backup coming," she blurted out, hoping to distract Austin. She had to do something to get that gun barrel away from Clint's head.

"Oh, do ya now? Did Clint here get through on a cell phone?"

"Yes, he did, and there will be cops swarming all over this place within the next few minutes." Her voice held more mettle than she felt.

"Boss, maybe we better get out of here," the third slug chimed in.

Austin shook his head and jabbed Clint in the shoulder with the pistol. "He's bluffing. His odds of getting through on a phone line way out here are slim to none. Why do you think I leased this place?"

"But maybe he got lucky. Maybe that sheriff is on his way. They know who we are—"

"They won't be telling anybody."

Lacy saw the gleam in Austin's eye and her heart stilled again. She couldn't lose Clint—she had to draw the gun away. She had to do something to distract Austin. His hand gripped the gun more tightly and her attention flew down to Clint who was looking up at her, watching her with steady eyes—probably willing her to control herself.

Or watching for the right opportunity to strike back. She knew he needed her to distract them…. If she drew the gun, they had a chance.

Clint's eyes hardened; steam practically started rolling from his ears and he shook his head oh so slightly. "No," he mouthed, but she'd already started screaming…and she knew he was reading her thoughts. She knew she could distract them. She yanked hard against Austin and continued screaming. Her adrenaline spiked, she saw Cigarette-butt looking panicked. Felt Austin shift against her and she screamed louder and squirmed violently.

Austin's hands were full, holding her in one arm and holding a gun on Clint. Though she was screaming she registered that he was a control freak or he'd have let Cigarette-butt hold the gun on Clint.

"Woman!" Austin exclaimed, rewarding her screams by pointing his pistol straight at her. "Be still or you'll get the first bullet."

"Lacy, be still." Clint's voice was soft, drawing her gaze, quieting her screams.

The gun was at her temple, she could feel tremors racing through Austin's body, knew he was near breaking but felt no fear. She felt only love looking at Clint.

For a moment she'd succeeded and drawn the gun away from Clint. Only to see the now-alert Cigarette-butt level his gun on him.

"Austin," Clint said, his words tight, clipped, "take the truck and go before the sheriff gets here. You can still get away and you won't have harmed anyone. You do not want to harm Lacy."

"Why? I'd be doing the world a favor getting rid of this magpie."

Clint frowned. "No. You wouldn't." He slowly started to stand.

"Hold it right there, buster." Cigarette-butt snapped, jamming his shotgun into Clint's shoulder. "Nobody told you to move. Shoot her, boss, and let's get out of here. Carl, load up," he snarled at the man Lacy had decided didn't have a brain of his own. Carl practically ran to the truck and hopped inside.

Angered, Austin pressed the cold metal harder against her temple and she could see the fury building in Clint. Her pulse screamed at high speed, fearing he was about to get himself shot. Shifting toward Austin, she focused on the control freak in him.

"Who's the boss here?" she asked, cutting her eyes at him. "You or Smokin' Joe over there?"

Austin grimaced. "Shut up. Dawson, we aren't going anywhere until I say so."

Dawson. He finally had a name.

"Look, we got plenty of cattle sold," Dawson snapped. "I ain't hanging around here so some officer can waltz up and handcuff me. I ain't goin' back to no prison 'cause you won't admit it's time to call it quits."

"Yeah, boss," Simple Simon chimed in from the cab. "Daw has a point."

"I give the orders here!" Austin yelled. The air rang with fury as he pushed Lacy forward so he could step toward Dawson. Lacy lost her footing and stumbled, catching Austin off guard. He yanked her back but it was too late. Losing his footing, they both tumbled forward.

Clint rammed his elbow into Dawson's gut, then lunged for Austin. She was knocked to the side as Clint locked on to Austin's arm, one hand on the gun, one hand around his neck, pushing him back as they wrestled for control of the gun. Lacy started to get up to help, but Dawson shoved her from behind and sent her sprawling toward the side of the trailer.

She caught herself before running into it, spinning around just in time to witness Dawson slamming the butt of his shotgun into the back of Clint's skull. The sound reverberated with a sickening thud and Lacy's whole world tilted as Clint's knees started buckling and his hands fell limp and lifeless to his side. "Clint," she cried out, reaching for him. In that terrifying instant, watching him fall forward, her life flashed before her eyes.

What if I never have the chance to tell Clint I love him? What if Clint died because of her stupidity? *Oh, dear Lord, what have I done?*

What if he were already dead?

Clint fought back the darkness overcoming him as he hit the ground. Searing pain ripped through his skull.

"No!" he heard Lacy scream, and he forced his head upward. It felt heavy and the effort was daunting. Blood ran like a river into his eyes as he tried to focus on Lacy. He found Austin standing above him, gun leveled down. He saw Dawson turning toward Lacy's voice, then to his horror, he saw Lacy evade Dawson's reach and throw herself at Austin.

Like a wildcat, tears streaming down her cheeks, she clawed at his face. *Dear Lord, she was beautiful, and faithful.* He knew she would fight till death if she had to.

Clint struggled to regain his senses; he had to help her. Austin shoved her back. Yet, tough as nails, she belted him in the nose with her elbow. Staggered by the force of the blow and bleeding profusely, he tottered away from her, his gun dangling dangerously in his hand.

Clint focused on the gun aimed at the woman he

loved. Determined, he willed his limbs to move, tried to shake the blackness swallowing him. Then Dawson stepped into view, now with two guns aimed at Lacy.

"Lacy," Clint called and, with all the strength he possessed, forced himself up. He propelled himself toward her, trying to draw the fire from the thugs as the darkness engulfed him.

The gunshot was the last thing Clint remembered.

Chapter Seventeen

Clint awoke with a start. Lacy.

Where was she? His surroundings came into focus and he realized he was in a hospital. Ranger's hospital.

A nurse stood at the foot of his bed studying a chart. His head throbbed like a jackhammer, but he struggled to sit up. He had to find Lacy. Had to know if she was alive—

"Hold on, big guy," the nurse said. Coming to his side, she gently pushed him back onto the pillow.

"Lacy," he whispered, his voice gravelly. His head was spinning.

"She's in the waiting room. The doctor has gone to tell her you are going to be okay. We stitched up your wound and the scan showed no other damage to your skull. You were very lucky, though you could have some short-term memory loss. But that's yet to be seen. You'll hurt like thunder, but you'll be fine in a few days."

She was alive. She wasn't harmed. "Thank you," he managed. Drained, but thanking God that Lacy hadn't been shot, he relaxed against the pillows.

A few minutes later the door opened and Lacy stepped inside. He drank her in, wanting nothing more than to see her safe. She was pale, her eyes were huge and he could see her body tremble.

"Clint," she whispered, moving to his side. "I'm sorry. So sorry."

"For what," he rasped. "You saved me."

She started to cry. "No, Brady saved us. He got there right after you passed out. He shot Austin in the hip." Silent tears streamed down her beautiful face. "I nearly got you killed. If I hadn't jumped on the back of that trailer…then I— I couldn't keep my mouth shut." She hiccupped and rubbed at the wetness on her face with the back of her hand.

Clint forced himself up on an elbow, wanting so much to hold her. "You were only trying to help." He reached for her and she came into his embrace willingly. Her tears wet his shoulder until the nurse returned and berated him for sitting up.

Reluctantly he leaned back against his pillows and watched Lacy attempt to dry her eyes with a tissue the nurse handed her. Reaching out, he clasped a wobbly hand over hers.

"I'm going to marry you," he said, more certain of the prediction than he'd ever been about anything in his life.

Lacy gaped at him, disbelief etched upon her face. "You said…I—" she gasped through her hot tears "—remind you of your mother, and I almost got you killed." Abruptly she turned and started to walk away.

Clint stopped her, holding tightly to her hand. "You do, sugar," he said, gently tugging her back to his side. "I didn't know what I was doing that day in your kitchen. My insides were going crazy and my heart was tripping out on me. You scared me." He paused, fighting back the emotions welling within him.

"But I've figured some things out since then," he continued. "I had planned on coming over today or yesterday—I've lost track of time. I'd planned on making everything up to you, but I got a little sidetracked."

Lacy lifted her head. The hope in her eyes melted any reserves he may have held. This was his woman. His gift from God.

And he was going to keep her.

"No." She pulled her hand away and took a step back. "No, I can't."

"Lacy. What's wrong? What do you mean no?" He didn't like the look in her eyes.

"This will never work." Lacy spun toward the door and he would have lost her had he not held firmly to her hand, determined to never let her go.

"You don't need to love m-me Clint." She sniffled and tried to compose herself. "You're right. With the way my personality is, there is no telling what I'm going to wake up and do tomorrow. I tried to come here and carry out a promise I made to God and I couldn't stay faithful to even Him."

"Now, hold on there." Clint tugged her to sit beside him on the hospital bed. "What do you pray every time you end your prayers?"

Lacy didn't understand what he meant.

"You pray for God's will to be done and not yours. I've heard you pray many times, and you pray that every time. Don't you?"

"Yes." Lacy stopped crying. "I wanted my coming to Mule Hollow to be about God and not about me."

Clint lifted his hand and gently rubbed strands of hair off of her damp cheek. "This isn't about you, Lacy. Not in the way you think. I've watched you, and I've seen your heart, and you've changed me. I had shut God out of my life and hadn't even realized it until I saw your relationship with Him.

"This was about me…and everybody else that has watched you in action. You might get a little carried away at times, times I've come to love observing, but your heart is true. You may not want your personality compared to the apostle Peter's, but, Lacy, just like God knew Peter's heart, He knows yours. He knows how true and faithful your heart is. And so do I."

Lacy shook her head and buried her face against his chest again. His words reached deep inside of her. Had her pride and her desire to let God use her in the way she saw fit overshadowed the *real* reason for His leading her to Mule Hollow? Could it really be true?

"Lacy," Clint murmured in her ear, "you are my answer to prayer. I've needed you for so long. I love you, Lacy. And if you'll marry me, I promise that we'll work together to fulfill the vision God gave you for Mule Hollow."

Every thought Lacy had deserted her when Clint said he loved her. She looked up and met his smoldering brown gaze. Slowly she touched his cheek with her trembling fingertips.

Light seeped into her veins, flooded her heart and a smile burst to her lips.

"Could you really love me, even after all I put you through last night?"

In answer, Clint leaned in and kissed her. The kiss was slow, strong and steadfast and chased away any doubts she might have had. When he lifted his head, his eyes were twinkling.

"Like I said before, the trouble with you, Lacy Brown, is you don't know when you're whupped. Will you marry me?"

In that moment she knew Clint had been right. They had been wrought for each other by the mighty hands of God to balance out their different personalities into a perfect union.

"Oh, Clint, I love you, too. But look where I got you with my stupid, impulsive actions. Why, I couldn't even keep my smart mouth closed when I had a gun stuck to my back. Clint…I could have gotten you killed!" Overcome with uncertainty, she buried her face against his chest and wept.

"Yeah, you could have." His voice was gentle as he smoothed her hair with his hand. "I have to tell you, Lace. I've never seen anyone braver than you. All the while, knowing you would make yourself the target of their frustrations, you stood up to those guys. They didn't know what hit them when you started screaming. *I* didn't at first." He pushed her away from him and lifted her chin so she had to look at him. "I wouldn't ever try to hold you back, Lace. I just want you on my team."

Lacy melted at his words; hope and pure joy surged through her. "Oh, Clint," she sighed. "I thought God brought me here to be the matchmaker. And He was pulling the strings all along."

Clint loosened his hold on her and cocked his head to the side. "Imagine that."

Clint nestled her against him and in the sweet silence filled with awe at their decision, Clint's heart changed.

"Lacy," he said, "Will you come to New Orleans with me?"

"I'd go anywhere," Lacy sighed against his cheek. "Any special reason?"

Clint thought of the letter he'd stuffed into his jeans pocket earlier that afternoon. "I need to see a lady who lives there. I need to invite her to a wedding."

Epilogue

Lacy stood with a small crowd on the corner of Main Street. Her heart was thumping with wild anticipation as she watched the moving trucks pulling around the corner. Glancing up, she smiled at Clint. He immediately drew her near, under the shelter of his arm.

"Look, Lace, it's what you envisioned," he said, bending close to her ear. "They're coming."

Lacy thrilled to the warmth of his breath against her skin. It delighted her soul to look around the small crowd waiting to help the three schoolteachers move into their new apartments.

Molly Popp, now a Mule Hollow resident for three weeks, had attended church faithfully every Sunday since moving to town. That told Lacy that she'd been right in coming.

Lilly Tipps also stood on the edge of the crowd beside Norma Sue. Lilly had been hurt by her ex-husband when he abandoned her upon learning she was pregnant, but Lacy felt an irrepressible spirit in Lilly. Looking down Main Street, it hit Lacy that she'd felt that same spirit in Mule Hollow when she'd first sat in her pink Caddy and felt that whisper of hope calling to her. It was a feeling of being down and out, but of not giving up. Lacy had a feeling that Lilly would never give up. And she knew just the ladies to give her support.

Scanning the rest of the crowd of familiar faces she had come to love, Lacy wanted to shout aloud for the hope she felt surging all around her.

You are so good, Lord. You are an awesome God!

"Can you believe it?" Esther Mae said, clapping her hands together. She hugged her husband, Hank. "I told you this plan was going to work. I told you."

Hank raised an eyebrow. "You were right. And I'm glad of it. You ladies did a mighty fine job of reviving the town. Looks like this just might work."

"Well, sure, it'll work," Norma Sue said. "You men had the doubts, we women knew the Lord had it under control all the time."

Laughter burst around Lacy, and she couldn't help it—she spun out onto the street with her arms open wide. "Come on, let's go welcome the newest residents of Mule Hollow."

Clint grabbed her hand, and together they walked down the center of the street toward Adela's apartments.

She and Clint had traveled to New Orleans and he had started a new relationship with his mother. She would be attending their wedding in March. Wedding.

"What's with the dreamy expression?" Clint asked, tugging on her hand.

"I was thinking about God's sense of humor. Just think about us—we came from standing on this street clashing heads together, to preparing to walk down the aisle together in marriage."

"I like God's sense of humor." Clint stopped walking and pulled Lacy into his arms. "I can't wait until you are Mrs. Clint Matlock." And then he kissed her.

"All right, that's enough of that, you two," Norma Sue said. "We've got things to do and there's no time for dawdling."

"Hey, Lacy," Bob called from where he'd taken the lead, "What's next on our plan for Mule Hollow?"

"Oh, now it's *our* plan," Esther Mae harrumphed, then she smiled. "That's just like a bunch of men to join in after the fact."

"Well, I was thinking," Lacy said, glancing at the colorful buildings lining the street. "We've got the ads out and women are coming, but so is winter. We might just need to be patient. We can't expect Mule Hollow to turn into a metropolis overnight." Suddenly an idea started to bloom. "However, I bet we could do a Christmas or Epiphany pageant of some sort."

"You mean acting?" Andrew asked, frowning.

"Cowboys acting in a play," Lilly added. "I'd have to see that to believe it."

"I was thinking that you could be in it also."

"Me." Lilly stopped and stared openmouthed at Lacy. It was that look Lacy knew so well. "Do you know how large I'll be in a few months? Why, I'm getting round so fast that my shirts are going to be screaming mercy soon."

"Yup, I know. You'll be just right."

"I don't think so—"

Clint tapped Lilly on the shoulder. "You might as well give up. What Lacy wants, Lacy gets."

"I told Clint that," Sheri added. "So you might as well get ready. If Lacy wants you in the play you'll be in the play. Baby and all."

They had reached the vans and the teachers were stepping down from the cabs. Immediately, the cowboys went over and offered their help. There was a lot of promise in the air.

It made Lacy want to sing.

So she did.

"Love is in the air…Mule Hollow, where all your dreams come true…"

* * * * *

Dear Reader,

I'm so glad you decided to join me on this wild and wacky ride with Lacy Brown! From the moment Lacy popped into my head, driving that pink Caddy and talking my ear off, I knew I was in trouble. A good kind of trouble. Her zeal for God made me want to draw closer to the Lord in my daily walk and to seek His will with all my heart. She made me want to let my hair down, too, and have some fun. She made me laugh—and that was a very good thing for me at a time when I really needed to smile. I pray you had as much fun as I did and that God blessed you in a special way as you read Lacy's story.

Lacy so wanted to please God—I believe ministry is the way to do that. I hope if you aren't involved in some type of ministry in your church or community that you get involved with one. You'll be blessed through your involvement and be a blessing to someone at the same time.

Until next time…keep smiling, seeking God with all your heart and reaching out to those around you.

Blessings,

Debra Clopton

Love Inspired SUSPENSE

RIVETING INSPIRATIONAL ROMANCE

Coming in October...

STORM CLOUDS

by Cheryl Wolverton

An urgent call from her brother, a former secret service agent whom Angelina Harding hadn't seen in years, brought her thousands of miles to Australia. Only to find him gone. And it was only with the help of his friend David Lemming that Angelina had a hope of finding him.

Steeple Hill®

Available at your favorite retail outlet.
Only from Steeple Hill Books!

Take 2 inspirational love stories FREE!

PLUS get a FREE surprise gift!

Mail to Steeple Hill Reader Service™

In U.S.
3010 Walden Ave.
P.O. Box 1867
Buffalo, NY 14240-1867

In Canada
P.O. Box 609
Fort Erie, Ontario
L2A 5X3

YES! Please send me 2 free Love Inspired® novels and my free surprise gift. After receiving them, if I don't wish to receive anymore, I can return the shipping statement marked cancel. If I don't cancel, I will receive 4 brand-new novels every month, before they're available in stores! Bill me at the low price of $4.24 each in the U.S. and $4.74 each in Canada, plus 25¢ shipping and handling and applicable sales tax, if any*. That's the complete price and a savings of over 10% off the cover prices—quite a bargain! I understand that accepting the books and gift places me under no obligation ever to buy any books. I can always return a shipment and cancel at any time. Even if I never buy another book from Steeple Hill, the 2 free books and the surprise gift are mine to keep forever.

113 IDN DZ9M
313 IDN DZ9N

Name	(PLEASE PRINT)
Address	Apt. No.
City	State/Prov.	Zip/Postal Code

Not valid to current Love Inspired® subscribers.

Want to try two free books from another series?
Call 1-800-873-8635 or visit www.morefreebooks.com.

* Terms and prices are subject to change without notice. Sales tax applicable in New York. Canadian residents will be charged applicable provincial taxes and GST. All orders subject to approval. Offer limited to one per household.

® are registered trademarks owned and used by the trademark owner and or its licensee.

INTLI04R

©2004 Steeple Hill